Money, Money, Money!

THE
SEAGULL
LIBRARY OF
GERMAN
LITERATURE

HANS MAGNUS ENZENSBERGER

Money, Money, Money!

A SHORT LESSON IN ECONOMICS

TRANSLATED BY SIMON PARE

WITH ILLUSTRATIONS BY SONAKSHA IYENGAR

LONDON NEW YORK CALCUTTA

This publication was supported by a grant from
the Goethe-Institut, India.

Seagull Books, 2022

First published in German as *Immer das Geld*!
© Suhrkamp Verlag, Berlin, 2015

First published in English by Seagull Books, 2020

English translation © Simon Pare, 2020
Illustrations © Sonaksha Iyengar, 2020

ISBN   978 1 8030 9 212 6

British Library Cataloguing-in-Publication Data

A catalogue record for this book is available from
the British Library

Typeset by Seagull Books, Calcutta, India
Printed and bound by WordsWorth India, New Delhi, India

CONTENTS

I

A VISIT FROM AUNT FÉ

'She's coming!' It was Fanny who made this announcement. Cheerfully, triumphantly almost, she brandished the extra-wide postcard of an Alpine panorama. Everyone at lunch immediately understood whom she meant.

'Aunt Fé,' my mother mumbled and held the spoon high above the soup tureen with a sigh.

My father eventually broke his silence to ask, 'When?'

Little Fanny crowed, 'This evening!' and waved the green-inked scrawl in the air as evidence.

Aunt Fé's missive didn't mention what business she had being at a Swiss cog railway station in early April. She liked to keep her messages succinct, and the postcard was her preferred means of communication with the outside world. 'It's cheaper and less awkward than the telephone or these new-fangled machines I find so suspicious.'

My whole family knew that she owned an estate on the shores of Lake Geneva around a legendary villa with a terrifyingly large number of rooms. We did have a Swiss phone number for her, but whenever my father tried calling, all he got was a housekeeper's dismissive voice announcing 'La Pervenche' into the receiver. None of us knew what this name meant. Dad had looked it up in the dictionary once and found out that it meant 'Periwinkle'. I imagined the man on the phone to be a butler of the kind I was familiar with from English films. In any case, all he would say was that 'Madame' was not available.

She was apparently on one of her trips again. This time, not in New York, Lisbon or Buenos Aires but on a small mountain excursion.

'Periwinkle!' I cried. 'We decorate salads with those.' In my godmother's eyes, I was the most sensible person in the entire Federmann family. Yet I knew as well as anybody that it was pointless to argue with her when she'd got one of her idiosyncratic plans into her head.

My brother Fabian, who has already outgrown me despite being three years younger, immediately interrupted. 'Felicitas,' he declared, 'you're just annoyed because Aunt Fé's cleverer than you are.'

'Oh, stop it,' Dad said. 'Can't we even enjoy lunch in peace?'

Yes, once more the atmosphere in our household was electric. Mum was wondering what she could make for dinner for an aunt who would hardly be satisfied with something as simple as meatloaf. Fortunately, it was Thursday. Our Polish cleaning lady Bozena came once a week. She isn't someone you fool around with either. She battles dirt as if she had a personal vendetta against it, and occasionally smashes a vase or lampshade in her ongoing war on grime. There's no question of sacking her, though; she's been cleaning our house for many years and is so incredibly loyal that we'd never dare get rid of her. Even Mum realizes that, although she does get worked up about every scratch Bozena leaves as her imperishable mark on heirlooms such as our coffeepot. We all rush out of our rooms when she moves in with her mop and bucket. She's always chiding us for leaving clothes or toys strewn across the floor. You have to hand it to her, though: she's always willing to help out in an emergency and that includes serving at a dinner. Of course, she doesn't declare such work because she refuses to sign any forms or pay social insurance—she wants cash in hand. She sends the money home to her sick sister and feckless brother who live somewhere near Krakow.

Maybe it's worth mentioning Aunt Fé's appearance and general demeanour. She must have been a great beauty once. She flashes you a saucy look from an old photo in our family album as if she wouldn't say no to a little flirt, but she must be well over eighty-five now. She won't divulge any further details about her age. With the exception of her housekeeper or butler, she lives alone in her villa. My father reckons she probably has a gardener and a chambermaid too. He must have lifted that from a nineteenth-century novel—I really doubt that there are still chambermaids bustling around in white aprons nowadays.

I went to the theatre once to see a Russian play about a tyrannical old woman who was only ever referred to as the 'Lady General', even though there was no general to be seen. That lady was the spitting image of Aunt Fé. She would rap the floor with her cane when she got angry, and the cane had a silver top shaped like a lion's head that looked terribly familiar. My godmother is in the habit of leaning on a similar stick.

If she doesn't wish to hear something, she'll play deaf, yet as soon as anyone tries to recommend that she get a hearing aid, she'll shout them down in a jiffy. She doesn't like being argued with on principle. My parents walk on eggshells around her—they don't wish to provoke her wrath.

Aunt Fé is anything but miserly. Whenever she comes to visit, she will give Bozena a generous tip. She's always asking us how much pocket money we get, enquiring if it's enough and what we do with it before slipping us a few notes. I've noticed that she always has some foreign money with her—francs, pounds or dollars. She once gave me a hundred Danish kroners, a yellow note with an appearance more impressive than its actual value. When I took it to the building society, they gave me less than fifteen euros in exchange.

Mum doesn't much appreciate Aunt Fé's way with money. Behind her back, my mother speculates on where her fortune comes from, if it was honestly gained or whether she inherited it from one of her husbands.

'Who knows how those people came into their money in America?' It's a rhetorical question no one answers. 'Fé spoils not only our children but Bozena too. And yet she's never enquired how Franz and I are getting by.'

Dad says nothing; he prefers to steer clear of this kind of conversation.

It was a rainy April evening when Aunt Fé pulled up outside our little house in a black limousine. The driver put up a large silver-coloured umbrella and escorted her to the front door. She was carrying only an embroidered handbag and a bottle of champagne, and the first thing she said was, 'You don't need to worry that I'm going to descend on you. I'll be staying at the Four Seasons as usual, and in a few weeks I'll be gone.'

Dinner went off surprisingly peacefully. Our guest was in a good mood and had second helpings of the starter.

'How cosy it is here,' Aunt Fé marvelled. She didn't appear to notice that we didn't have any champagne flutes. She did, however, shower unusual praise on my mother.

'You don't know how lucky you are, Franz,' she told my father, referring to the recipes from Budapest that were my mother's legacy from the Austro-Hungarian

Empire. We had veal medallions with steamed dumplings, and *Kaiserschmarrn*—sugared pancakes with raisins— for dessert.

After dinner, Aunt Fé lit a long Virginia cigarillo to go with her coffee. 'I hope you don't mind, Friederike,' she said. 'Would you happen to have an ashtray?'

Dad knew where such a thing was to be found, although he was never allowed to smoke indoors.

Out in the hallway, after saying goodbye to her dear relatives, Aunt Fé rummaged in her handbag and distributed some banknotes to the three of us. She did the same for our birthdays too. Each time, one of us would find an envelope bearing the name of some hotel or other in our letterbox.

Emerging from the door, she rapped her cane on the step, and her driver immediately started from his nap, raised the umbrella and ushered her to the waiting car.

I've no idea what my parents discussed next because we were immediately sent to bed. Fabian and Fanny didn't want to go to sleep, so they both came into my room.

'No one actually knows who Aunt Fé really is,' Fanny began. 'She probably isn't our aunt at all.'

'Surely you don't believe she's Dad's sister,' Fabian said. 'She's far too old for that.'

'Then she must be our great-aunt,' I said. 'Same difference. Leave Aunt Fé alone. Maybe she just likes us. What I do know is that she doesn't have any children of her own. OK, that's enough. Now get out, please. I want to go to sleep.'

This all sounds as if it happened a long time ago, but it feels like yesterday to me. That's because this family visit was not the end of the matter. Aunt Fé, who had little time for the Federmanns' domestic routine, had a surprise in store for us the very next day. She invited us to her hotel and 'us' didn't include our parents—just Fabian, little Fanny and me. It was less an invitation than a summons, delivered to our home by courier.

'Be careful!' Mum warned. 'It's best not to tangle with that old dragon. She'll start ordering you around. And we could tell you a story or two about her mood swings, couldn't we, Franz?'

Dad merely mumbled something and wandered off to his desk.

Everyone always called her Aunt Fé, but her full name is Felicitas, like mine. She'd insisted that I be named after her, despite my mother's objections. Mum thought it ridiculous that all the names in our family have always begun with an 'F'. It was only much later that I found out that our great-grandfathers had been called Friederich or Ferdinand Federmann, establishing a family tradition. The in-laws also had to comply with this rule and baptize their children accordingly; they could count themselves lucky if the occasional 'Ph' appeared on a birth certificate, as in my grandfather Philipp's case. There is supposedly even a very distant cousin of ours called Philine. I haven't

a clue why the Federmanns adhere so strictly to this stupid rule. In any case, there was nothing anyone could do when Aunt Fé rapped her cane on the floor and announced to my father that she demanded to be my godmother. And that is how I got my name.

Aside from this one foible, however, everything about the Federmanns is completely, not to say tediously normal. We live in a semi-detached house that Dad bought many years ago. It's in a residential area on the outskirts of town, and the mortgage hasn't yet been paid off in full.

So far, so just about bearable. Fabian, Fanny and I aren't the offspring of complicated third and fourth marriages, like most of the other kids at school, but of outrageously orderly circumstances. I do sometimes wonder about the safe, almost square environment in which I've grown up. We are what is known as a 'nuclear family'. This model is clearly on the path to extinction to judge by the number of patchwork families in our neighbourhood. The children come with ex-wives and ex-husbands, and there's even the occasional step-sibling and adopted child involved.

We're very contented with our normality. Even the intervals between our births seem to have been lifted from a family-planning guide. I'll soon turn eighteen, Fabian's in high school and Fanny's just started primary. She detests the fact that lessons start when she feels she should still be in bed. She's cheeky, imaginative, impatient and forthright. This stands her in good stead at home, although Mum often tells her off. Just like Fabian, she values the little comforts that help her to pass the time. She has a tiny radio she loves to turn up full blast so we all get to hear her favourite music—a mixture of '80s outlaw country and Sunny Rocket.

Fabian, on the other hand, looks incredibly grown-up at the tender age of fourteen and likes to fiddle around with his brand-new white phone; he must always have the latest model. However, he does know his way around the fuse box in the cellar and can tell all the different makes of car apart. I think secretly he's quite into money, but he'd never admit it.

There's only one problem that mars our otherwise harmonious family life: for some reason, our money never quite stretches until the end of the month, even though our father has been toiling away for years as a specialist at the vehicle registration office; or, to be precise, in Division III of the Ministry of Transport; or to be even more precise, in Department 2 of the Driver and Vehicle Licensing Agency. That's the kind of jargon civil servants use when they're together.

I don't believe a certain kind of car owner ever makes it as far as Dad's office. By that I mean those who beg for very specific sets of letters so that they can bomb around the streets with licence plates like HYPE, MIZZI or ROY. Whoever's in charge of allocating number plates might be easily tempted to give someone their preferred combination in exchange for a surreptitious plain envelope. Dad wouldn't put up with that kind of nonsense, of course. If the name on the door is Franz Federmann, then bribery is not an option.

He has a guaranteed income and cannot be sacked. I've no idea whether he's a civil servant or not, but whatever he is, his salary is always transferred to his building society account on time. Mum receives a steady amount for household expenses and a personal allowance. None of us has what might be called a luxurious lifestyle. It isn't right, Dad says.

Until Fanny's birth, Mum brought home a second income. She used to work part-time in an organic shop that sold wizened apples and strange-smelling herbal teas. Dad gives extra lessons to the beginners at his chess club, and he brokers all kinds of insurance for his colleagues, for which he takes a commission, I believe. Most people are afraid, and so it's easy to foist more and more insurance policies on them. They're no use if you feel constantly insecure, though. Fabian also supplements his pocket money by repairing our neighbours' lawnmower or dishwasher.

Despite urging us to be thrifty, Mum loves shopping. That must be because she was born a Ferenczy—so her maiden name also begins with an 'F', which is thoroughly appropriate. When she was little, her parents spoke Hungarian at home, but now she's only just about capable of saying *viszontlátasra*, or 'goodbye'. She was married once before, as a very young woman, to a minor official in Budapest, but that only lasted for a few years. He looks anxious on his passport photo. He clung on to his job at the agriculture ministry, but she wanted to emigrate to Germany as soon as the border opened. So she walked out on him and filed for divorce. She brought with her a few peculiar expressions she'd picked up from her parents. For instance, she would say that you should always dress 'befitting your rank', even if you didn't have any money.

I think that's why she enjoys clothes shopping so much. Yet another scarf or a new blouse, and then she tells everyone that they were 'massively reduced'. She believes in bargains. She's a sucker for a special offer.

'They reduced this raincoat by 60 per cent!' she says. 'Which means I saved 120 euros.'

'Oh, think it through, Friederike!' Dad remarks. 'Sixty per cent of what? First they stick some unholy price on the label, then they cross it out, and every time you fall for the simplest of cons!'

This only makes her angry, so Dad prefers not to comment on her purchases.

Our parents' conversations on this subject get on our nerves. We intervene when things turn really stupid, leading to exchanges like the following.

'Do you have to keep arguing about stupid money? Receipts, bank statements, ring binders and bills, the whole time! I guess it's our fault for costing so much! "The mortgage, school expenses, class trips. Trainers and rucksacks," you always say. The list goes on and on.'

We really should have held our tongues. Mum is incredibly touchy on this topic, and Fabian, who comes up with some smart remarks if and when he can be tempted out of his reserve, only adds insult to injury.

'That's normal,' he explains.

'It isn't normal,' cries Fanny. 'It's boring.'

'Normal and boring,' I interject in an attempt to reconcile the two parties. 'It's normal that everyone talks about money. We're not the only ones. You only have to listen to people yelling into their stupid phones in the subway or in cafes. It's normal that we don't have enough money. It's normal for our parents to argue about money, and it's just as normal that it annoys us and we get angry about it. We should all be like Dad. Whenever a conversation becomes too dull, he simply tunes out.'

For ages I didn't understand why my parents never criticized Aunt Fé. Mum only ever picked her to pieces behind her back. It was only quite a bit later that Dad took me aside one evening to tell me a secret.

'You should know that Fé isn't your aunt: she's a fairly distant great-aunt. And, by the way, she isn't just well off, she's rich—filthy rich.'

'Aha!' I said. 'So that's why everyone tiptoes around her. Because there's an inheritance at stake.'

'You'd be better off keeping that thought to yourself,' he advised. 'Inheritances aren't just tricky, they're a disaster. You can't imagine what happens when a family is buried under an avalanche of money. The bickering can turn bloody.'

The day of our invitation to Aunt Fé's arrived.

'You know the Four Seasons. It's right in the centre. You don't need to take the bus—my driver will pick you up.'

We were familiar with the car with the tinted windows, and the hotel concierge was already informed.

'In the penthouse,' he said. 'The Executive Suite.'

The lift boy took us up. Her rooms were bigger than our entire house. Aunt Fé had ordered a pot of tea for herself.

'What would you like?' she asked. Fanny wanted ice cream, Fabian a Coke and some biscuits, and I settled for tea.

'How was school?' Aunt Fé asked. Then, without waiting for an answer, she continued, 'I've heard outrageous things about what goes on there. It's criminal what they teach children today! Nothing but chemistry, geometry and Latin. Fiddle-faddle! Teachers don't have a clue about economics because they're on salaries like your father, receiving their money every month—or to be more precise: receiving what's left of it. They don't notice the deductions. So many deductions: all kinds of taxes, so-called social insurance contributions, specific insurance premiums, telephone bills, electricity, water, heating, health insurance, the television licence fee, and God knows what else. And you know what the net amount is? The paltry remnants of their salaries. No wonder you can't make ends meet!'

We had no idea how to respond.

'Why are you ranting?' grumbled Fanny, tucking into her ice-cream sundae. 'Money, money, money! Why does everyone make such a fuss about it?'

But I was eager to know more, and Fabian pricked up his ears too. 'If you have time, Aunt Fé, you should tell us how money works. You're bound to know more about it than Dad or Mum.'

'I only ever drink Earl Grey at this time of day,' she replied. 'Milk has no business whatsoever in tea. A couple of drops of lemon juice and that's it. Now . . . if you're interested in economics, fine. Money is a complex subject, though. You would have to come and see me often.'

'No problem. As often as you want,' cried Fanny, who liked the hotel because we could have anything we desired.

'But you'll have to pull your weight. I'm going to give you an exercise to do, and you must write down your thoughts for next time.'

'More homework,' groaned Fanny. 'Just what I need!'

'No one's forcing you to come. You two don't mind writing a few sides, do you?'

'Of course not,' I said.

'Well then, we have a deal. Here is the first question: Where does money come from? Write down whatever pops into your mind. I'd like to hear your answers next time. Shall we say the day after tomorrow at half past four? My chauffeur will drive you home. Give my regards to Franz and Friederike.'

As soon as we stepped through the front door, we were asked how our visit had gone. None of us wanted to spill the beans, since it would only have caused trouble, not least due to Aunt Fé's withering analysis of school. We all pondered what to say at the next meeting. Only Fanny, who'd never been to a grand hotel before, couldn't resist pestering our mother with enthusiastic reports about the fabulous room service.

Everything at Four Seasons was just as it had been the first time. Aunt Fé greeted us in a sort of Indian dressing gown embroidered with peacocks.

Fanny put her hand up first. 'I know where money comes from. My father takes it out of the building society. If you have a card, it comes out of a bank machine. You just need to know the right number. Every adult gets one of those cards. Children are the only ones who don't.'

Aunt Fé gave a lopsided grin and said nothing.

Fabian didn't agree. 'That's because you don't have an account with credit on it. If there's nothing there, then the machine won't spit out any cash. The third time you try, the machine swallows your card and you're left empty-handed. You really think the building society gives Dad presents? Here's what I've written:

Where does money come from? My father says it's obvious—his money comes in regularly from the city council or the state. Some government depart-ment or other pays his salary every month. Other

WHERE does the **MONEY** come from ?

people work for a company, and what they earn goes into their account. Otherwise, it might come from a person who owes somebody money or as a gift from someone. Or from the social security department. You can also inherit. But I don't think Dad understood my question properly, so I held up a 10-euro note in front of his face and said, 'Look at this carefully. There are lots of initials on it: BCE ECB EZB EKT EKP. There's also a number and a year and an illegible signature. You go to the office every day for notes like this! That's so weird.'

He freaked out. 'Count yourself lucky,' he shouted. 'It pays the mortgage and the electricity, and your dentist and for new shoes, and all the rest of it . . .'

I tried to calm him down. 'You're absolutely right,' I said, 'but I'm not talking about money for living costs. What Aunt Fé wants us to tell her is where money comes from in general.' He merely grinned before saying, 'Oh boy, she's given you a fine nut to crack there!' That was all he said. He probably didn't want to admit that he had no idea himself.

Fabian read this from his exercise book and, despite the occasional stutter, I it sounded pretty good.

Aunt Fé nodded too. 'Good, Fabian. If you would like a snack, please be my guests! Just tell me what you want. So what do you think, Felicitas?'

I was far from satisfied with what I'd heard so far. 'You're oversimplifying things,' I said.

'Of course. You always know better,' Fabian cried.

Rapping her cane on the parquet floor, Aunt Fé barked, 'Read it out!'

'OK, then. I think that money hasn't always existed.'

'How do you know that?'

'Let her read!'

'The cavemen we know from local history lessons and films didn't have money. They were hunters and gatherers, and later farmers who grew the staple foods they required. So it must have been a few thousand years before money was invented. But who came up with the idea first? Historians are still arguing over that. Some have dug up coins and examined them. Others have travelled to speak to indigenous peoples, *índios* or bushmen. It turns out that these people once used shells, cows and daughters to exchange things of which they had too much or too little. There was a lot of trade in slaves too. In the long run, however, hauling humans, animals and objects back and forth or finding buyers for brides was too inconvenient. It probably caused lots of arguments too. How many goats were you supposed to pay for one woman?

'So, to make barter simpler, some people began to hoard small and particularly valuable things. Pearls, for example, or gold. Things you could put in your pocket. I read somewhere that the Phoenicians made a fortune by making coins from rare metals. As if! Who believes that?'

'No, you're right,' said Aunt Fé. 'We need to believe in money or it doesn't work. What would we do if the greengrocer on the corner said, "What? Am I meant to give you my lovely chanterelle mushrooms for that ridiculous scrap of paper? Do you realize how hard they are to find? People go out with baskets into the forests of Poland because they know where to find them, and others wait in the nearest town to buy them as soon as they arrive. Fresh mushrooms must either be dried or taken straight to the central market. They're perishable. And eventually, they arrive at my corner shop."

'That's what the fruit-stall owner argues. Imagine the earful you'd get if he didn't believe in money. He'd laugh you out of town. "You must be joking," he'd say. "You can stick that blue stick of paper where the sun doesn't shine. Any old Tom, Dick or Harry could come in here waving a 20-euro note, but how do I know it'll be worth anything tomorrow morning?" '

'What are you talking about, Aunt Fé? No one's ever said anything like that to me. This isn't the black market! Anyway—I haven't finished yet.'

'Please carry on, Felicitas.'

'So . . . Nowadays, we get our money from the bank of issue. That's the highest bank of all—well, in Europe at least, which is why it's also known as the central bank. The letters on the banknote are its initials. Its headquarters are in Frankfurt, and it can print as many banknotes as it wants. They call it "money creation"! Sounds grand, doesn't it? From absolutely nothing they make something pretty valuable.

'Now, they always say on television that the bank of issue is independent, but I don't believe them. They're only pretending. In fact, the government, business leaders or trades unions or other banks pressure the central bank to keep on printing. If there are rumours of too little money in circulation, the central banks have to press the button and produce more banknotes. And conversely, when there's a glut of money and everyone has too much, the bank has to slam on the brakes. That creates a shortage. They don't only do that in Frankfurt but in America too and anywhere else in the world with a central bank. I've no idea who dreamt the whole thing up.'

'Not bad,' said Aunt Fé, who had just taken a sip of her first sherry. 'Do you know what? The gentlemen from the bank of issue—and they're always men in dark suits—don't have a clue what money is, although they talk of nothing else. I once met one of those so-called governors in Basel. Every few months they all get together in a concrete tower near the station, all hush-hush, at a place called BIS—another one of those abbreviations the moneymen hide behind. But I'm wise to them: BIS stands for Bank for International Settlements. It's the central banks' central bank. It's been around for a long time. It was established immediately after the Great Depression of 1929, and since then has never moved from that tower in Basel, whatever else might be going on in the world. In the middle of the Second World War, leaders from America and Europe and the rest of the world met there and negotiated peacefully with the

Greater German Reich about "international settlements". Nobody really knows what schemes they came up with—and the BIS continues its machinations to this day. Up or down with interest rates, the dollar or various quotas. If someone could be a fly on the wall at those meetings, he or she would have it made the next day. But those gentlemen have the whole building swept for bugs every now and then, and they keep mum so that not a word gets out.

'As it happens, one of them invited me to dinner back in the days when the deutschmark still existed. He was called Dietmüller or Tietmeyer—a tall, good-looking, white-haired man with a receding hairline. He was president of the German Bundesbank in 1996 or '97. Ages ago. Back then I was full of beans and up for all kinds of pranks. Over dessert—crème bavaroise, it was—I asked him point-blank, "So what is money?" He was so discombobulated he almost choked on his food! Then he cleared his throat and said that it was very, very hard to define. First, one had to answer the following questions: How do the amounts of money M1, M2 and M3 differ? Furthermore, one must not confuse endogenous credit money with term money, bank money and subsidies. Digital money was even more complex. In a word, he had no idea what he was dealing with. And he isn't the only one. Saint Augustine was once asked what time was. Well, he replied, as long as no one asks about it, we all know what time is, but as soon as someone wants further details, we're incapable of saying. It's the same with money.

'We can of course ask the economists, since they lecture on the subject. They've come up with all kinds of theories. Unfortunately, though, they cannot agree, and so they can never explain precisely what happens when we order a pizza or fancy buying some mushrooms.'

Fanny was only listening to our discussion with half an ear—she spilt some more ice cream on her blouse while leafing through a chunky French magazine, gazing at the latest models of ladies' boots—and Fabian raised his hand again.

'None of that really matters,' he said. 'Who cares about definitions? Money was a stroke of genius, and that's why everyone copied the idea. There isn't a single country on earth that doesn't use money.'

Fanny lowered her magazine and asked, 'But why is there never enough of it?'

'Ah, let me explain,' Aunt Fé said. 'If there's more money around than things to buy with it, then it is no longer worth anything. It's simply a piece of paper, and no one will lift a finger to earn such scraps. I was in Bolivia a few years ago, although for the life of me I cannot remember why. You know where that is, of course. In South America. The banknotes had zeros all over them and were worth so little that you had to place them in bundles on a set of scales to pay. For a kilo of peso bills you could get a small maize loaf, that's all. Tell me, Fabian, how much does it cost to send a letter?'

'No idea. Who writes letters nowadays? I only ever text or email.'

I was better informed than he. 'Sixty-two cents.'

'Oh yeah.'

'Yet stamps keep going up in price, year after year, as do subway tickets, electricity and everything else.'

'What did it use to be like?'

'There were still pfennigs back then.'

'Those don't exist any more. It's cents now.'

'And how many pfennigs are there to a cent?'

'You want us to do mental arithmetic now, Aunt Fé?'

This was too much like hard work for Fanny.

'About double,' I said. 'One euro is worth 2 marks. Easy-peasy.'

'Not quite,' Fabian exclaimed. '1.955 and a few more decimals.'

'You know-it-all!'

'Stop it! Both of you.' This was Aunt Fé again. 'When I was little, it cost 12 pfennigs to send a letter. But my father lived through the 1920s and the incredible financial rollercoaster ride. The currency went up and down all the time. At first he stuck a groschen on his letters— the equivalent of 10 pfennigs—then it was suddenly 20 marks and a year later it was 100 billion. That's more zeros than you could ever imagine. The envelope was plastered with stamps. Inflation was rampant, just like in my Bolivian example. That's what happens if a bank of issue prints more and more money.'

'It becomes worthless.'

'Correct. If you're a good printer, with the right paper and the right machines, and you make your own euros or dollars, the police will come after you and throw you in jail. That's Section 146 of the criminal code: "Whosoever counterfeits money with the intent that it be brought into circulation as genuine or that such bringing into circulation be facilitated, or alters money"—and so forth—"shall be liable to imprisonment".'

'Excuse me, Aunt Fé, but how come you know the criminal code by heart?'

'I had a friend who got locked up from time to time. A delightful man, but jinxed. So stay clear of that business, you hear! Only politicians are allowed to print counterfeit money. Some experts call it "fiat money".'

'What does that mean?'

'It comes from the Bible, which you've probably never read. Genesis 1—a book about the creation of the world. In the third verse of the Latin version, God says: "Fiat!" Not the car manufacturer but: "Let there be." From nothing He creates heaven and earth. The central banks didn't need telling twice. They also create something from nothing—money.'

'And why do they do that?'

'Every state comes up with a good reason, especially when they're facing bankruptcy.'

'Surely countries can't go bust.'

'They have more elegant terms for it. They merely cease payments. Then there's "restructuring" or debt conversion. It is a very common procedure.'

'I don't believe you.'

'Oh, Felicitas. Five years ago, a few valiant Americans found out how many times it had occurred in the past. Reinhart and Roloff or Rogoff or something. Look it up on the Internet if you don't believe me, you know how forgetful I am. But if I remember correctly, in the twentieth century alone, Brazil and Chile didn't pay their debts seven times, France eight times and Germany three. And the Greeks have supposedly been insolvent for half the time they've been independent from the Turks.'

'So why do governments go on borrowing more money?'

'Because they want to be re-elected, so they quickly raise pensions. Or because they start a war. Or due to high unemployment, or because people have taken on too much private debt.'

'And what do they do after that?'

'Exactly the same thing that large companies do with their financial statements. There are a thousand tricks for reducing one's debts. One thing never changes, though: every citizen, including babies and little old ladies, is liable for all the borrowing and has to pay the interest on it. By official calculations, that amounts to over 2 trillion euros. That's 25,000 euros per head, but there are some countries where a person is already hundreds of thousands in the red before he or she has even wet their first nappy.'

'So how do you get out of a debt trap like that?'

'Oh, that's no problem. There are various recipes. If a country has its own currency, it can devalue it at the stroke of a pen. If you go to the bank of the exchange bureau the next day because you're planning an overseas trip, your own currency is suddenly worth far less and you receive fewer dollars or kroner in return. That's galling, but it does make *some* people happy—exporters. All of a sudden they can market their cars or machines abroad at a lower price and make better deals. Then the next cycle begins. The next country devalues its currency, putting its neighbour in trouble.'

'But that doesn't eliminate the debt!'

'Of course not. But it looks better if, for example, you cross out a few zeros. It's called a currency reform. There have been quite a few of them in Germany, but Italy and France have also shrunk their currencies a few times. Debt relief is another method. The bankrupt state is let off a few billions, and a few people who were stupid enough to lend it money are left empty-handed. Someone is always out of pocket.

'Those, however, are some of the more extreme measures that states take when they have no other option. Nowadays, most governments are a little more subtle. They say, "A little inflation isn't so bad!" That way, their citizens may not even notice their money dwindling away. At least 2 per cent per year: central banks don't merely allow it—they positively demand it. So inflation is always carefully planned. Dutiful savers are offered an interest rate below inflation, only to realize after paying their taxes that the amount they've set aside is shrinking with every passing year. People in the industry tend to call a spade a spade, and this is known as "financial repression". Every state does it. They intoxicate themselves to the point of bankruptcy. Anyway, that's enough for today. What would you like to do for next time?'

'Oh no, more homework!' Fanny wailed.

'If that bothers you, you needn't come,' said Aunt Fé, shaking her cane at my sister. 'This isn't school. There are no marks or detentions or reports here. You don't need to bring along any books either. The only thing I'm interested in is what's inside your heads. If any of you finds that too boring, you can stay away. Next Tuesday each of you will tell us a dream. It would be best if it were about money, for that appears to be of at least some interest to you all. I don't mean the loose change I send you home with. I mean more, far more than I can ever give you.'

As usual, Fanny would have preferred to make no effort. 'You can't choose your dreams—they just come. I only ever dream of ants or some other creepy-crawlies.'

'Then tell us about them,' said Aunt Fé. 'It's still better than homework, don't you think?'

Even before we reached home, we had started to argue over this new game. Fabian claimed that he sometimes dreamt of a red sports car. Overhearing this, the chauffeur broke his silence.

'I'd leave well alone if I were you—they're nothing but trouble. You can see for yourself that this country is peppered with No Entry and speed-restriction signs, and if you're not careful, they take your driving licence away. If they give you one in the first place, that is!'

'You're absolutely right, Herr Forster,' I said. 'And anyway, everyone should keep their dreams to themselves. But we do have to think up something for Tuesday or Aunt Fé'll be cross with us.'

'I don't know why you're so keen on going to see her,' my mother said at dinner. 'Just because she has a chauffeur and invites you to her expensive hotel. You'd be better off concentrating on your schoolwork. What do you say, Franz? I think your aunt's merely showing off to our kids.'

'Firstly, she isn't my aunt and secondly, she wishes us all well,' my father shot back. 'It really won't do the children any harm to hear something different for a change.'

I didn't feel like listening to this conversation, which always ended the same way. Fabian and Fanny went to bed while I played on my phone for a little longer.

At the next meeting, Fabian was the first to present his dream. 'Something really weird.'

'Good!' said Aunt Fé. 'Go ahead, I'm listening.'

'I was sitting in a plane. It was a little biplane. I was surprised at how easy it was to steer, even though I'd never flown a plane before. It was as easy as riding a bike.

Such an amazing feeling! I flew a little lower and stuck my head out of the window into the wind. I spotted an unfamiliar city below me and circled nonchalantly over the market square. On the seat beside me was a silver briefcase. I knew precisely what was in it, so I put my hand inside, grabbed a handful of green banknotes and chucked them through a small hatch beneath my feet.'

We were all on the edge of our seats, even my god-mother. Maybe I was surprised or even a little jealous of my younger brother for showing such mettle.

'Hang on,' I said. 'Whoever heard of a plane with a hole in the floor? Do you know what I think? Fabian's sitting at the controls as if he were on the loo! He doesn't want to help the people below—he just wants to shit on them!'

'Let him finish, Felicitas!' I knew Aunt Fé would soon start waving her cane. I had to allow Fabian to carry on. I couldn't compete—I hadn't dreamt at all in the past few nights.

'Well,' he continued, 'the money tumbled down like a shower of confetti. I kept throwing heaps of notes out, and saw more and more people streaming into the square. The whole city was out in the streets. It was funny the way they scrabbled about and squabbled with one another. Suddenly my briefcase was empty, so I chucked that out too, past the church spire. Then I accelerated and tried to fly away, but the engine began to stutter and I saw the propeller spinning slower and slower. "What's going on? Maybe I've run out of fuel. Help!" The aircraft began to fall, slowly at first and then faster and faster. In my nosedive I could make out every single tile on the roof of the city hall—and that's when I woke up.'

'That's precisely the type of story I wanted to hear, Fabian. Very well done! What about you two? What nice dreams do you have to tell us? Come on, out with them!'

'I've forgotten,' Fanny mumbled. I couldn't think of anything to say either.

'I think Fabian was very generous—at least in his dream. He gives away all his money, and to total strangers as well. He enjoys it. It's as easy as flying. Such an amazing feeling! The more money he tosses away, the happier he is. He even throws out the briefcase. That might have been a bit over the top, though, because he had none left for himself in the end. He ran out of fuel, so to speak. Suddenly he was broke, no longer flying high.'

I considered the situation for a minute and then dared to contradict her. 'I'm sorry to say this, Aunt Fé, but if you want to help someone, you should first study them carefully. You have to take them seriously, or you won't have a clue what they really need. That's what Fabian doesn't understand. After all, the only thing his dream demonstrates is that he thinks he's a high-flier. He's literally chucking money out of the window. He doesn't actually want to help those people. They look tiny to him, like ants. He almost dies laughing when he sees them brawling and tussling over the money. Then, when he runs out of banknotes, he gets scared and calls for

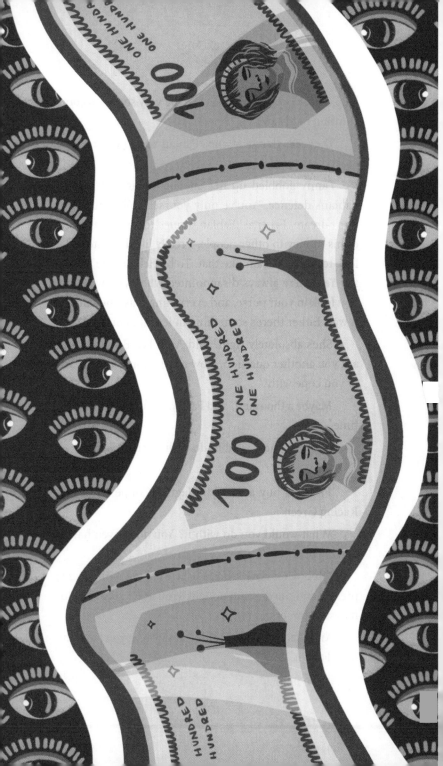

help. Those people would have to be very stupid to come running to his aid.'

They all glared at me. Fabian said nothing and looked offended.

Fanny gobbled up her chocolate bar and rose to Fabian's defence. 'You've only yourself to blame if you don't dream, Felicitas! Fabian *wanted* to give away some of his money to other people. I really liked his story. I'd love to have a dream like that. To be rich and be able to fly! Yet you're always disappointed when you wake up. You look in your purse, and everything's just the same as it was. Either there's something in it or it's empty.'

'She's absolutely right,' said Aunt Fé. 'But I'd like to ask you another question. How much money could each of you cope with?'

'Maybe a thousand,' said Fanny. 'That'd last me a long time.'

'A lot! I'd know what to do with it,' cried Fabian.

'Like what?'

'First, I'd buy an F-Type Jaguar Coupé in British Racing Green.'

'What would you do with it? You don't even have a driving licence.'

'Oh boy oh boy! It has a 5-litre engine with a compressor and can go from nought to 60 in 4.5 seconds. But it costs a ton of money.'

'And then what? How little imagination you have, my dear Fabian.'

'If there's any left, I'd invest it shares that bring in money.'

'What do you think of that, Aunt Fé?'

'Let your brother have his little dream! How about you, Felicitas? You'd prefer to keep a low profile, my dear?'

'Because I know what happens to all those unsuspecting people who have a windfall or win the jackpot in the lottery. Most of them can't cope and come to a wretched end.'

'Do I hear sour grapes or the voice of reason?'

'I wouldn't object to 50 or a 100,000. I'd be able to study in Cambridge or Yale and blow the rest.'

'See, this game's much more fun than Ludo or Monopoly. Try it on your friends. It will drive them crazy because each person will give you a different answer. And you, Felicitas, have once again spoken with wisdom beyond your years. You scored less well for your dreams, mind you. Come along with some better ideas next time.'

'What? Another exercise?'

'Who knows how much longer I'll be able to enjoy the pleasure of chatting with you. For as long as I'm around, though, I'm going to keep you on your toes. For next week, look around your bedroom and draw up a list of all the items in your drawers and cupboards and where they come from.'

We went obediently on our way.

The next time we appeared at half past four on the dot at the hotel reception, Herr Stäuble, the concierge, greeted us like regular guests.

'Madam is expecting you.'

This time there were various kinds of truffle—nougat, marzipan, chocolate, rum and many others—in Aunt Fé's suite. But before we could present the lists we'd brought along, she said, 'My dears, guess how many people work for you?

'Our parents maybe, and Bozena.'

'I'm going to prove to you that it's over a million.'

'I don't believe you. The only people who come to our house are the postman or someone like that.'

'Did you look at where the things in your rooms come from? From China, Turkey, France, Morocco, Bangladesh. Didn't you notice? Where do your toys come from? The cups, shoelaces and scissors? If you make a list of all the things you need on any normal day, you'll see that it runs to many pages.'

She waited until each of us had taken out our lists. But instead of asking us to read them aloud, she changed the subject completely.

'Do you know what the Germans believe? That they're world champions—not just at football but also at exporting. The newspapers and television are always trumpeting how many billions our exports earn for the country. The automobile industry, the mechanical engineering firms and arms manufacturers are constantly setting new records. Imports are also on the rise—and not simply because the supermarket on the corner has avocados from Peru, sushi from Japan and apples from Chile. You buy lots of other things from all over the world. Where do you think petrol comes from, or gas or copper? Those are imports, and they cost a pretty penny too.'

'You told us to write down what we found in our bedrooms.'

'Oh, really? So you don't have electricity? How do you heat your house? What does your father put in his car? I'd also like to know what you did at autumn half-term.'

'We were in Turkey. By the sea, so we could go swimming.'

'Aha! Have a guess how many people you employed there, Fanny.'

'Why me? The plane was full.'

'I'll list all the people who looked after you. The woman at the counter who checked in your little suitcase, the man who searched your bag and asked you if you were carrying a bottle of lemonade, the police officer at passport control, not to mention a few hundred other people you never laid eyes on. The air traffic controllers, the cleaning team in the toilets, and so forth—and you haven't even made it to your seat on the plane yet.'

Fabian knew the details. 'It was a small Airbus. A twin-engine 319.'

'Really? And who built it? A few thousand more staff. I'm telling you, on that one day, you were reliant on several hundred thousand people doing something for you.'

'But they wouldn't even have noticed if we'd stayed at home. They couldn't care less about us.'

'Of course not. They're not doing all of those things for *you*. They're only doing them because they're paid to. That's the wonderful thing about money. I sometimes think that it is in fact the greatest invention of them all.'

'But lots of people are paid for doing things which don't benefit us one bit.'

'Civil servants, you mean. People like your father, sitting around in a government department somewhere.'

Fabian wasn't going to let her get away with that. 'He makes sure people don't drive around in rusty old cars with broken fan belts and worn-out brakes.'

'It's sweet of you to defend him, my dear, but lots of ministerial executives produce nothing but piles of wastepaper, fodder for pen-pushers and shredders. The same is true of journalists, solicitors, equal-opportunity officers, estate agents, publicity freaks and bankers. The bigger the office, the less valuable the job they do.'

'But they earn more than other people.'

'Do you know who makes money fastest? High-frequency traders. Those gamblers behave as if they're in the Wild West. The quickest on the draw wins, and time is calculated in milliseconds. Only those with the biggest computing capacity have a chance—everyone else loses. So be careful, Fabian, if you want to play their game!'

'It sounds like those shell-game players who con their classmates out of all their money.'

'Speculators are far more cunning. They play for such tiny amounts that you don't even realize you're being swindled. Yet they shift such massive sums around the market—up to a third of worldwide turnover, I believe—that they earn a sizeable amount even if each operation generates only a pfennig of profit.'

'Half a cent, you mean.'

'Oh yes! You see, Fabian, my knowledge is all second-hand. It's been a very long time since I myself had a flutter.'

'None of this has anything to do with us,' Fanny grumbled.

'You're right. So let's talk about potatoes instead. Guess how much a farmer receives for a kilo of potatoes? Barely a quarter of what you pay in the shop.'

'I think that's terrible.'

'So do I.'

'I don't,' our aunt announced, 'and I'd like to tell you why. Because of the division of labour.'

'What's that?'

'Something wonderful. Just imagine if you had to do everything yourself! Grow bananas, print newspapers, sing operas, take care of the sewage treatment plant so you don't drown in sludge.'

'I'd rather not!'

'It's all very well saying that now, Fanny, but wait until you're eighteen and you have to consider what you're best at. Every one can do something another person cannot. In any case, everyone can do something better than you, and vice versa. that's why there are so many different professions. I had a look around your neighbourhood once. Three houses away from you lives a tenant who's written what he does on the nameplate beside his doorbell. You'll be amazed what it says: *Hohlmüller, sound-maker*.'

'That's a strange job.'

'What's stranger is that, walking past his house, you don't hear a single sound. What on earth does he do in there all day?'

'Making sounds. As if there wasn't already enough noise around! Patrol cars with flashing blue lights and wailing sirens. Pneumatic drills. Hooligans. Souped-up sports cars like that green Jaguar of yours, Fabian.'

'You're the last one who can complain about noise,' I reminded Fanny, 'with your radio on full blast. Always playing Sunny Rocket or Ariana Grande!'

'We were talking about the division of labour,' said Aunt Fé, refusing to be drawn away from her topic. 'There are crazier jobs. A Dolomite beater, for instance, or mining blaster or upholsterer—no one has any idea what they do. There's a specialist bridal hairstylist here in the hotel, who will only serve people who are getting married. And that's without mentioning the thousands of totally superfluous professions.'

'Who do you mean? Beggars?'

'Oh, they've always existed. Begging is an honourable profession. No, I mean jobs like equal-opportunity officer or high-frequency trader.'

'Oh! Or those busy-lizzy presenters on television. No one would miss them if they were done away with and never replaced.'

'You're not thinking hard enough, children! Imagine if you had a garden . . .'

'We do, in front of our house, but it's tiny.'

'What grows there?'

'The neighbours have complained because it's so untidy. They'd like us to iron the grass with the lawn-mower, but the mess just happens. The plants do whatever they want. Look away for a few days, and the whole place is overgrown.'

'That's exactly like the division of labour. It isn't only the beautiful and the useful that thrive, but weeds, nettles and thistles too. Some plants are actually toxic! But would you feel like ripping them out every day?'

'I wouldn't.'

'You see. It's the same with professions. It's incredibly difficult to abolish something pointless, like the death penalty or the atomic bomb. We haven't even managed to get rid of the permanent wave and the tie yet! When I was a child, I had to wear a sort of uniform for my first communion on Divine Mercy Sunday, and a wreath of flowers. My mother insisted on the finest bobbin lace from Plauen. The photographer made me pose with a big

fat candle in front of a painted backdrop, and clamped my neck in a brass brace so I wouldn't blur his picture. I think those gadgets still exist. Most practices and customs are as obsolete as gout—and just as hard to eradicate.'

'But what about luxury?'

'Oh, that's completely different. Luxury is essential.'

'I'm sorry, Aunt Fé, you just claimed we'd be better off without ties. Then you could also get by without those fabulously expensive handbags.'

'I'm disappointed in you, Felicitas. I hope you realize that we can trace the origins of our prosperity back to luxury? If it weren't for charcoal burning, there would be no glass and no porcelain, and without the carriage, no car. Someone had to pay for the expensive craftsmanship or it would never have grown into an industry.'

'I imagine that if it weren't for the French Revolution, those developments would've quickly run out of steam.'

'Right again! I'm amazed by how much you know, Felicitas. I can tell you one thing, though: waste is essential. You will admit that much, won't you? Think of restaurants! There's a three-star chef on the ground floor of this hotel.'

'And a McDonald's next door.'

'I'll tell you why. In the past, you had to carry your own provisions when travelling. In the Middle Ages, there was only the occasional miserable hostelry where you could count yourself lucky if they laid a bundle of straw on the ground and gave you a bowl of bread soup—and even then, only if you had enough thalers or guilders on you. No one but the upper classes could afford decent cuisine—counts and bishops and a few rich merchants. I've heard there were 75 confessors at the French court and 3 examiners of the King's stool.'

'What did *they* do?' Fanny asked.

'Even kings sometimes need the loo. No wonder that the palace stank and everyone wore perfume—and not just the ladies. And when His Majesty had finished, an expert had to inspect the privy to check that all was well. But that was nothing. The other lackeys had far more work to do, for example the many people working in the kitchens. A whole brigade of cooks—those in charge of soup, roast meat, fish or vegetables, not to mention pastry chefs and dishwashers. There was a specialist for every dish. And what happened when the French beheaded their king? Overnight, those hordes of people were out of a job. An army of unemployed servants.'

'So what?'

'As you know, the Revolution was also good for business. In every coup, there's always someone who makes money. The nouveaux riches wanted fine things to eat, but their wives didn't fancy cooking. They preferred to go out and that, my dears, is how the restaurant came into being. Delicatessens, bistros and cookshops sprouted up everywhere. But enough discussion for today. Are you hungry? It's on me, of course. Where would you like to go? To the three-star chef or the chip shop?'

Aunt Fé's anecdotes had exhausted us, and we were happy to go along with her wishes. Even Fanny fancied lobster bisque and coq au vin instead of pizza for once. I couldn't stop her ordering a crêpe Suzette to round things off either. It would probably have made me sick, but she polished it off with no trouble. She's only seven but she has a bigger appetite than I do.

Our next meeting with Aunt Fé had to be cancelled because she was indisposed. I know what that means—she wasn't poorly; she simply didn't feel like it. My suspicion is that she was lounging in bed with a novel. She likes reading doorstoppers.

Incidentally, Herr Semmelschneider rang our house on Friday. He's the tax consultant who takes care of Dad's paperwork. Dad has to hand in a tax declaration every year because of his small secondary jobs and because Mum earns a little on the side.

'I'm sorry, Herr Federmann, but there are still a few details that are a little vague and we need to clear them up.'

Semmelschneider is a mousy man and I can't stand him, but he does know what he's doing because he used to work at the revenue office. He's now retired, I think, or maybe they kicked him out. The aim of the meeting was to see if Franz Federmann could deduct anything from his taxes.

'No, we won't have any luck with your study here. The taxman won't take that into account. There is further training, though! You need to keep up to date. Seminars, courses! And what about services around the house?'

'Well, we did have to call the locksmith once because Fanny spilt the contents of her school bag. A hundred and thirty-nine euros including travel expenses and VAT.'

That's approximately how their conversations go.

All these pernickety calculations put my father on edge. One question after another: 'Do you have all your receipts to hand? Extra income from the chess club? Insurance commissions? And what about your wife? Accrual or separate estates? How much did she earn from her part-time job at the organic shop? What retirement and pension schemes do you have? I must look up about potential one-off payments. And you don't need to worry that I might take German tax laws lightly, Herr Federmann! One has to distinguish very clearly between (a) earnings (b) the sum of the receipts (c) total receipts (d) income (e) taxable income and (f) income after tax.'

Such talk makes my dad's head spin. Bozena's name must never come up during this Punch-and-Judy show, of course or Semmelschneider will frown and refer to illegal employment. 'We don't want to run the risk of an audit! We'll sort out the documentation somehow, don't you worry!'

He rubs his hands together like a sympathetic confessor and sets to work straightening everything out on Dad's ancient computer. Later, he sends a detailed bill. None of us is allowed to disturb Dad under any circumstances until the tax consultant has gone.

I've noticed that Fabian takes a genuine interest in this ridiculous business. 'Once Semmelschneider has left,' he says, 'it's better not to ask Dad how it went. He gets annoyed if I do. He shows me the decisions and the forms and asks if I'd like to have a look at them. No way! I don't want to get all flustered. It'd be pointless anyway, because I don't earn any money, so the taxman can't take anything from me.'

Grandpa supposedly said before the Second World War that the highest rate of income tax in 1914 was 9 per cent. What about now?

'Guess how long I've been working for the revenue office?' my father curses. How's poor Fabian meant to react to that?

He has to listen to the same tax sermon every time. 'I recently read that large companies such as Google, Amazon and co. pay practically no tax. They're based in Luxembourg or on one of the Channel Islands and lobby and use lawyers to ensure they get off scot-free. Do you think that's true?'

Fabian couldn't answer this question, but his father's mind had already moved on.

'No one,' he exclaimed, 'has ever thanked me for giving away a third of my salary! They don't just deduct taxes but the solidarity supplement, pension contributions, health insurance, long-term care insurance, additional insurance and the television licence fee as well. Factor in road tax, fuel duty, electricity tax and VAT, and I'm giving them over half of my earnings. I have to accept that, but getting constantly bawled out by the authorities is beyond the pale. They suspect everyone, and yet it's virtually impossible to understand the rules. Herr Semmelschneider deals with this crap every single day, and the directives and decrees are too much even for him. Yet politicians dare to talk of tax giveaways! They seem to think they can do whatever they like with money they pinch from us!'

One thing you have to hand to Fabian is that he's not afraid of a debate, so he contradicted Dad. 'In return for what you pay, however, we have a welfare state that makes sure no one needs to go hungry any more. And there's a minimum wage as well.'

'And how is an independent hairdresser supposed to pay that, eh? What happens to our jobs if major companies pack up and move abroad?'

'They've had a minimum wage in Holland and France for ages, Dad. Even Romania has one! And it's never throttled business, wherever it was introduced. You keep complaining about tax, so tell me whether you think the fire service is a waste of money? You don't have anything against motorways, universities or sewage works, do you? Or with getting a pension when you eventually give up dealing with vehicle licensing?'

Fabian will make a fine social democrat if he keeps this up. I've no idea how long he argued with Dad. When he'd finally calmed down, I said, 'Nice work, little brother. You put up a brave fight, but I've heard enough for the moment. I've got to make a presentation in chemistry tomorrow on the difference between aromatic and aliphatic bonds, so I'm going to bed now.'

The next week, our meeting was on again. Aunt Fé had clearly grown tired of pretending to be ill. I even rooted around in her bathroom to see if she'd been taking any medicine. No clues, not a doctor's prescription in sight. I presume she just wanted to read a nice fat book and enjoy some peace and quiet.

This time we found that tea had already been served and a sumptuous sundae awaited Fanny. Our hostess had even applied a touch of rouge. As she had neglected to set us a new exercise, she suggested a fresh topic.

'Whenever someone says, "Oh go on, you can trust me!" you know something fishy is going on. Remember that! They spend millions begging for your trust.'

'Who do?'

'Banks, political parties, companies, supermarkets. They plaster every surface with posters, place adverts in magazines and show commercials on television. Wherever you look, there's a little old lady in a blue apron, holding up some washing powder, a detergent or a miracle pill. During election campaigns, the candidates stare at you as if butter wouldn't melt in their mouths, wringing their hands and beseeching you. They only want the best for you. Or rather *from* you—your vote and your money. And why do they go to such lengths? Because they've tricked you so many times that no one believes them any more. I do hope you realize that.'

'You're always badmouthing politicians,' Fabian protested. 'You make out that they're to blame for everything.'

'Maybe they aren't,' said Fanny, 'but one thing's for sure—they're the most boring people on the planet. Whenever it's election time, they stick their faces up on walls and ask us to vote for them, but in reality it's just one politician trying to take another's place. It'd be better if they sorted out their arguments in private.'

'And you, Fanny? What about what you get up to in the playground? You and your friends ganging up on kids you think are stupid.'

'All because they're in the other class.'

'Who nicked little Paula's mobile?'

'What are you getting at?'

'That you're just like those politicians.'

'It's like a kindergarten in here,' said Aunt Fé, putting an end to the squabble. 'I often feel sorry for politicians. They have no choice but to fiddle and cheat. Some of them enjoy it, but if one has an idea and wants to achieve something, the others always put a spoke in his wheel. Everyone, from the backbencher to the leader of the parliamentary party, has to spend their time in meetings— one of the most tedious activities imaginable. No, the poor wretches have an unenviable job. Then, when things go wrong, they're bought off with a prominent position in Brussels or in waste disposal. It's a miracle that anyone agrees to enter such a ghastly profession.'

'Other people break their backs for 40 years in a vulcanizing factory or cleaning hotel toilets,' Fabian objected.

'And last time, Aunt Fé, you told us that we had to believe. If not, we wouldn't be able to rely on anything any more. Your own words! The fruit seller wouldn't give us any cherries ever again.'

'It wasn't cherries, it was mushrooms.'

'Who cares, Fanny.'

'I'd hate it if everyone was as untrusting as you.'

'Oh, you're so adorable, Fabian. I do like you. As long as it's trusting your parents or a friend, go ahead! Maybe you even have a teacher you can rely on, or a handyman who's mended your old bike a few times. They're all people you've put to the test.

'I simply don't want you to be fooled by the institutions that are continuously bombarding you with slogans. You shouldn't believe a thing they say. You can throw begging letters with a half-famished black baby staring into your eyes straight into the bin. However often they repeat their account number, they omit to mention their advertising costs. Do you know how much they spend on their own salaries, miscellaneous administrative costs and promotion? At least a third of their income. Some are greedier. Whoever they are, you watch out, Fabian! Trust is a rare commodity. Once abused, it vanishes without a trace and it's slow to return. I know what I'm talking about.'

'I think that's only half the truth, Aunt Fé. Look, I only need to pick up the wireless phone on your desk and call 112 for the fire service or an ambulance, and I can be sure they'll come. Our father recently rang the police because our neighbours were making a racket in the middle of the night. Within five minutes, a patrol car had pulled up outside, and they quietened down immediately. It didn't cost us a penny either.'

This isn't going anywhere, I thought, so I got involved. 'Yes, Fabian, that kind of thing sometimes happens. Once when we were ice skating, the ice caved in under a little fat boy because he'd gone too far from the shore, and a muscly man really did rush over to fetch him out, completely free of charge. It does happen. Look at this! A biro with Fritz Oschetzke Roofers, New Brandenburg, printed on it. The only thing is, I've never been to New Brandenburg and I don't know any roofers. A pen like this is abandoned property, adrift in the world. It is, incidentally, also the only area of life in which communism emerged victorious. You can ask anyone in the street for a light, request a glass of water in a hospital and go to the toilet in a café, all for free. So far, anyway. Mind you, they're now charging for the latter in railway stations, all because someone had a business idea for turning shit into money.'

'One euro-fifty. It's a total rip-off!' Fabian exclaimed.

'And yet you should take note of what Aunt Fé just said. Your fabulous phone is always offering you things that apparently don't cost anything. Surfing and flat rates, Skype, Twitter and God knows what else! Simple, flexible and all at knock-down prices. What a bunch of lies! Read the terms and conditions—the small print. It runs to around 7,000 words in Facebook's case. You'd be amazed, Fabian, at what you'd find there. Not only are they over-familiar, but they also say, "We reserve all rights not expressly granted to you." Of course, no one reads this sneaky declaration of submission all the way through—you probably signed it without looking as well.'

'Nicely put, Felicitas! I really don't understand why people are always fiddling with those bothersome things, nattering into them in trains, cars and out in the street. Talk about bad manners!'

'Just you wait, Aunt Fé, until that Herr Forster of yours breaks down or you faint. It can happen, even to you. Then you'll be glad I have my little phone.'

'I'd rather not know all the misfortunes you wish on me, my boy, just so that you can be my knight in shining armour. Until then you need to realize that not only is that web mafia trying to swindle you but so is every competition, every loyalty bonus, every voucher. I prefer to stick to the old proverbs for guidance, and one I heard as a girl was "There's no such thing as a free lunch". Well, not in this hotel anyway: they charge everything to my room.'

'Our parents are always saying we need to save up,' Fanny complained.

'I'm sorry to hear that. And what do you do if your money keeps running out?'

'We need to kiss some of our wishes goodbye,' Fabian explained. 'I'd like a new bike, but I can't afford one.'

Fanny thought for a second. 'My friend Lily could probably lend me a bit. She only has to ask her dad.'

TERMS AND CONDITIONS

10M 10M
8M 8M
6M 6M
4M 4M
2M 2M
1.5M 1.5M
1M 1M

WE RESERVE ALL RIGHTS

NOT EXPRESSLY GRANTED TO YOU

'You could, if that's true,' said Aunt Fé. 'Or you could do what your mother does. She recently gave me a twirl in her new summer coat made of parachute silk. She's probably paying for it in instalments or putting it on the overdraft, although they usually charge extortionate interest rates for that.'

'Overdraft?'

'When you spend more than is on your account. Forget it, it's far too expensive! But your mother's summer coat is a trifle. Imagine you'd like to buy a house one day but don't have enough money. What do you do?'

'No idea.'

'You do what Franz did. You go to the bank and take out a mortgage. Like a company that wants to grow or a factory in need of new machinery. Sign a stack of documents and the bank may grant you a loan, but only against collateral.'

'What's that?'

'You need something the bank can get its hands on— a piece of land, for example, or a steady income like your father's. Someone without a job will never get a single cent. They want to be sure that Franz can always pay his interest, but not only that—he also has to pay back a small percentage of what he owes the building society every year. It's called repayment. It goes on for decades, and the funny thing is that the house doesn't actually belong to the Federmanns, but to the bank. It's all in the contract. If it ever entered your mother's head to get divorced . . .'

'Mum would never do that.'

'How do you know? I don't wish to recall how many times *I've* walked out.'

'You must tell us,' I said. But Aunt Fé didn't want to.

'Well, let's assume Franz could no longer meet his mortgage repayments. The building society would pounce, and you'd be out in the street. That's the trouble with loans. In fact, the only people who get a loan are those who don't need one. The person you owe money to is your creditor.'

'We've been here before. This relates to trust and belief.'

'Correct. I did warn you—watch out or you'll be left in tears. What's wrong? You suddenly look very uncomfortable. Have I upset you?'

None of us was really satisfied with Aunt Fé's sermon about trust, credit, collateral, repayment and so forth.

'Fine. Let's think up something more fun for next time. I'd like to invite you to come on an outing with me next Wednesday.' She wouldn't reveal where we were going, though.

On our way home, Fanny said, 'What she said about getting divorced makes me sick. And building societies are outrageous. I don't want to hear this stuff any more.'

'No one's forcing you to come.'

But of course she came. Curiosity got the better of her.

We were very excited. Herr Forster and his big limousine weren't waiting to pick us up, as Aunt Fé wanted to try something different this time—a coach trip. She'd apparently asked Herr Stäuble where she might find such a strange vehicle. At the ZOB. Fabian immediately knew that this was the central bus station. 'We'll meet there, children. Here's some money for a taxi.'

Aunt Fé asked at the information desk when the next bus was scheduled to leave. 'Where do you want to go?'

'It doesn't matter.'

'There's one leaving for Klatovy in quarter of an hour.'

'Now where might that be?'

'In the Czech Republic. I don't know where exactly. Ask the driver.'

'Perfect. The three of you don't mind going on a mystery tour?'

I had to rush to the bank to change some money because once again Aunt Fé had only large-denomination notes in her handbag and nothing but Swiss francs. I brought her back some Czech crowns.

'They look a bit old-fashioned,' she said. 'Very pretty!'

We were the last ones to board. The bus was full. What were the other passengers like? I didn't see any tourists. Maybe pensioners, traders; women with headscarves and large, brightly coloured plastic shopping bags. There was also a bearded gnome who tried to sell us honey and hazelnuts—'100 per cent homegrown'.

The journey to the Czech border dragged on and on. Aunt Fé would have liked to explain the difference between money and capital to us as we drove along, but we were more keen on watching out for lynxes and beavers in the dense Bavarian Forest and promised to listen to her later. When we reached the barrier bearing a coat of arms with a white lion, two customs officials boarded the bus. They didn't have the slightest inclination to check our papers but merely loomed over a few Asian-looking passengers and demanded to see their passports and visas. Then, with a tug on their belt buckles, they waved us through.

On the other side, Fanny announced that she needed to get off the bus immediately. 'Is there a toilet here? I've got to go,' she squawked. We also needed some fresh air because the bus stank of garlic and sweaty clothes.

'Let's stay here then,' said Aunt Fé. 'I've never been anywhere like this before. We'll have a look around.'

I couldn't understand her enthusiasm because it seemed at first sight as if we'd ended up in some desolate backwater. A long line of roadside stalls were selling all kinds of tacky goods. Vietnamese hawkers tried to flog us fake watches and smuggled cigarettes. Fabian insisted on filming them on his new mobile. Three of them tried to tear the phone from his hands, backing off only when Aunt Fé brandished her cane at them.

Next we came to a dreary, boarded-up church, obviously the centre of this dump. The clock had stopped, and stinging nettles smothered the gravestones in the small churchyard.

A few burly men wearing black clothes and gold chains were smoking as they loitered at the only cross-roads. Fabian was fascinated by the women in doorways winking at him. They were dressed in quilted jackets, patent-leather boots with stiletto heels, fishnet tights and black miniskirts.

'That's funny,' he said. 'They've all got ponytails. And what huge earrings they have too!' It was immediately clear to him what was going on here. 'That's a brothel,' he told his younger sister.

Fanny asked Aunt Fé, 'What are we doing here?'

'You know your mother says I'm moody.'

'It's not true.'

'In any case, Friederike thinks I'm rash, and she may be right. Why else would I have brought you here? This place looks like the end of the world.'

'It was your idea, Aunt Fé.'

'True. I want to do more than just sit around in my villa in Switzerland or in hotels. I like to see something new from time to time.'

But Fanny was restless and hungry. There didn't appear to be any Bohemian taverns here, nothing but a grubby-looking Chinese basement restaurant advertised by a garish neon sign and called Royal Garden.

'So what would you like?' Spring rolls, chicken soup with coconut milk, Peking duck: the dishes on the menu were identical to the ones on offer at home.

Aunt Fé was ecstatic nonetheless. She though it was 'interesting' to drink a genuine Pilsner lager. She stared in disbelief at the moustachioed waitress who spoke nothing but Chinese. We had to tap on the numbers on the menu to order. When the bill came, the waitress waved away the credit card: she only took cash.

'Very sensible,' said Aunt Fé. She could barely believe how cheap everything was. 'A fraction of what it would cost in Geneva! They say the girls out in the street are amazingly cheap too. I asked the toilet attendant. Can you guess why?'

While Fanny polished off her sticky lychee juice, which the fat proprietor had personally served her, Fabian suggested that it was pretty obvious really. On the one hand, demand; on the other, supply. The price was the result of the interaction between the two.

'Oh yes!' Aunt Fé scoffed. 'That's what everyone says! That's what comes of listening to too many economists. But like most things they try to fool us into believing, it's utter nonsense.'

'Really? You've seen through their theories again, have you, Aunt Fé?'

'Think about it for a second. You saw how much a watch costs here. The price of a small beer. But a different one in a shop window in Zurich is supposedly worth 600,000 euros, even though it shows exactly the same time. Some artists sell pieces they've cobbled together in one afternoon for half a million, and one night in a simple suite in Dubai or on the Place de la Concorde can cost 20,000 euros.'

'Anyone who pays that much has only themselves to blame. It's the same with the price of flights, and I know what I'm talking about,' Fabian shot back, flaunting his expert knowledge. 'I can fly to Stockholm for 19 euros or I can spend 1,800 euros on the same trip.'

'It's no different with whores, only they used to call the expensive ones "cocottes". Now they call themselves "call girls" or "escorts". Some ladies sleep their way to the top, while others sleep their way to the bottom. So what do we conclude from that? Sorcery, luck or a scam? All three at once. But it always takes two to tango—one to pay and one to take the money. Many people long to ruin themselves and a love affair is often the cause. I could tell you some truly hair-raising anecdotes.

'Other people are compulsive collectors, desperate to own a particular stamp or a dog-eared 100-year-old comic. I know one man who built up a chain of bakeries by the sweat of his brow. He paid an astronomical sum for a heap of scrap metal a gallery owner palmed off on him. You'd be aghast at the sums some people spend out of sheer vanity! Have you seen that huge pile in Versailles? You wonder what the big idea behind that misshapen palace was. And what's the point of the victory parades in Moscow other than to allow the president to show off his medals and missiles? They couldn't give a damn how much it costs. It's all about making an impression.

'*Rational choice.* You understand English, Felicitas. You must have heard that expression before. It made the economists who coined it famous, and they seriously believe that people always act rationally, calculating everything down to the last penny and always opting for a bargain. It makes me laugh. Do you know anyone who really behaves like that?'

Aunt Fé took one last sip of her green tea, rapped her cane on the floor, took Fanny by the hand and walked out of the gloomy restaurant. All we could do was trot after her.

It was getting dark outside and it began to drizzle.

'I want to go home,' my little sister whined.

That wasn't quite so easy, though. The next bus back didn't leave until midnight, and there was no question of Aunt Fé taking an overnight bus.

'We'll find a comfortable hotel!' she said.

An awkward silence. I suspected that the best accommodation we'd find here would be a flophouse, and so it proved. We were directed towards a three-storey pre-fab tower block on the crossroads. Its rooms weren't intended for tourists and were rented out exclusively by the hour. Fanny was out on her feet and needed some sleep, so we followed a shaven-headed bouncer past two very, very young ladies to reception. There, a grey-haired matron wordlessly handed us two keys and pointed us upstairs.

Both rooms presented the same drab spectacle. The only furnishings were a narrow iron-framed bed with a stained blanket, a pink lamp, a jug of water, a thin towel and a decrepit bidet.

At this sight, Aunt Fé's expression suddenly darkened. She raised her cane menacingly and shouted, 'That's enough!'

I was familiar with these mood swings of hers. She could veer instantly from blithe curiosity to complete outrage. Having never experienced it before, Fabian was shocked.

The only one who seemed indifferent to Aunt Fé's fury was Fanny. 'My whole body's itching! I think there are fleas or bedbugs here. And it's cold. I want to go home!'

'She's quite right!' said Aunt Fé. 'I won't stay here a minute longer. We're going to take a taxi.'

'A taxi? Where to?'

'Home.'

'That'll cost a fortune.'

'So what!'

'You really think there's a taxi rank in this dump?'

This was the cue Fabian had been waiting for. 'Shall I?' he asked Aunt Fé, and before she could answer, he began fiddling around with his phone. It didn't take him long to find two taxi drivers in the provincial capital, one of whom even spoke German. Aunt Fé listened with amazement to his skilful negotiating. 'Please tell them we don't want one of those minuscule tin cans,' she warned. 'There are four of us.'

He announced triumphantly, 'I've got us a dark-blue Mercedes E Class from Klatovy. It'll be here in half an hour.'

'Nice work, my boy. What's the driver like?'

'I only talked to a hoarse lady at the agency.'

Outside it had stopped raining, and Aunt Fé had calmed down. She asked for a light from one of the girls in high heels waiting for punters and offered her one of her Virginia cigarillos.

The Mercedes arrived exactly 30 minutes later. The driver couldn't have been less like Herr Forster. He was skinny and had a clubfoot. Our aunt caught a pungent whiff of alcohol on his breath as he showed her into the car. There was also the obligatory pine-tree air freshener dangling from the rear-view mirror. Aunt Fé crossed herself as she got into the back. Fabian sat in the front, and I pulled Fanny closer; she immediately fell asleep.

Mirko, for that was the name of the clubfooted guy,· drove at terrifying speed. The customs officers knew him, but on the other side of the border he was flagged down by a policeman who demanded to see his papers and threatened to make him take a breathalyser test. It was only when Aunt Fé flashed the policeman a dazzling smile and handed him a business card that he agreed to let Mirko go. *Smugglers and dealers*, I thought, *should always be accompanied by a stately old lady*. That way they'd always make it through the Bavarian police's dragnet unscathed.

We didn't get home until six o'clock on Thursday morning. After Fanny had slept in, our mother took her aside and interrogated her. 'Why did you get home so late? What did you get up to on your outing?'

Fanny couldn't manage to repeat Aunt Fé's lessons about supply and demand because she hadn't been paying attention.

'Where did you spend the night?'

Fanny hummed and hawed, and probably cried a little too.

When my father got home, my mother confronted him with her findings.

'The girl was all over the place. She sobbed her heart out to me. You can't imagine all the things your aunt told the children! They left the country and went to a sinister place which even had a brothel.'

He must have shrugged helplessly when he heard this, but there's no stopping my mother once she's built up a head of steam.

'You'll never believe what she's tricked the children into believing.'

'What's that?'

'That we might get divorced.'

'Rubbish!'

'And what the bank would say if we did. That we might even lose our house. Aunt or no aunt, I won't stand for this. She's turned Fabian against the state too.'

'What makes you think that?'

'Because of taxes.'

It was this that made my father pull himself together and argue with her. 'Fé's remarks about the revenue office are spot-on, if you ask me.'

'All the same, I think Aunt Fé's gone mad.'

'Oh calm down, Friederike. Give her another few days and she's bound to leave.'

Although I didn't witness this conversation, I can guess how it went because ours isn't the only family that works this way. Anyone who has a family is accustomed to these things, and anyone who knows Aunt Fé as well as I do also knows that she'll soon have put our failed excursion out of her mind.

A week later she invited us to her hotel as if nothing had happened.

'It'd be better if you went to your singing lesson, Fanny,' my mother urged my sister.

'I don't have to go, Mum! Every time I sing out of tune or get stuck, the music teacher bangs his desk.'

'I don't like you skipping school.'

'Singing lessons are voluntary. I'd rather go and see Aunt Fé.'

This was one battle Mum couldn't win. For my part I wondered what Aunt Fé might have been dreaming up for this time.

It was a hot afternoon. Our hostess had turned on the air conditioning and ordered iced herbal tea. After some small talk about our parents and school, she returned to the subject of money, as always. This time, however, the question wasn't where it came from but how it smelt, felt and tasted.

'It's best if you've earned it yourself,' I claimed. This was pure provocation, because I guessed that most of the people who sat around this table, especially my aunt, lived off other people's money. Yet she didn't seem remotely bothered by this allusion.

'That's true. Money one has earned oneself tastes different to money one has been given or lent. One can let it melt on one's tongue like a chocolate. Debts or handouts can easily stick in one's craw. One should avoid them if possible. By the way, touch plays a part.'

'How do you mean?'

'One used to be able to handle money, because it was once solid, hard and heavy. Gold or silver. It didn't stay that way for long, though. In their day, the Romans were master forgers. They began by mixing a little copper, tin or lead into their coins, then it weighed less and less until there was nothing but a little gold leaf left on the surface. That's why people tended to put money in their mouths and bite it. It wasn't only forgers who had fun—do you know that counterfeits are known as "funny money"? No, emperors and sovereigns showed consistent ingenuity when it came to disposing of their debts. In the Thirty Years' War, the Kipper and Wipper celebrated a number of victories. They were small-time swindlers who manip- ulated the scales and knew exactly how to debase silver coins by adding copper, tin or lead.'

'How do you know all of this?'

'My dears, I once knew a man who hoarded Swiss five-franc coins because they were made of silver and the silver price kept rising until the metal was worth more than the coins. He had them melted down, and business was good for a time. Until the Swiss realized that copper, nickel and aluminium were cheaper. Since 1967, Swiss citizens have had to make do with alloys.'

'Like in East Germany! Coins got lighter and lighter there too.'

'But there they made do with aluminium! Currency became cheaper and lighter everywhere. An even more brilliant invention than coinage was paper money. Look at what it says on this!'

Aunt Fé fished a 1926 dollar bill from the depths of her handbag. I had to read out what was printed on it. 'Redeemable in gold on demand at the US Treasury.'

'The Bank of England promised something similar on its banknotes too. But it was a lie. I only hope you all know your *Faust.*'

'Of course. You have to pity poor Gretchen.'

'I'm talking about Part Two.'

'Never read it,' Fabian admitted.

'That doesn't surprise me, at your pathetic school. Mephisto knew what he was talking about, mentioning even then "the ghostly paper guilders". We used to learn such things by heart when I was young.'

And so, whether we liked it or not, we had to listen to a few verses from Aunt Fé's repertoire: ' "To whom it may concern: hereby be advised and told, / The present note is worth a thousand crowns in gold. / And in this general boon to ensure fair play, / We printed the whole series straight away: / Tens, thirties, fifties, hundreds— all are ready. / See how the people all rejoice already! / Such paper currency, replacing gold / And pearls, is most convenient: you can hold / A known amount." '[1]

Fanny groaned, but I had enjoyed Aunt Fé's dramatic recital.

'That's enough for now. Time for some refreshments. Or is it too chilly in here? I don't want you catching colds or your mother will be cross. We'll switch off the machine. It's nice on the balcony too. I'll allow myself a cigar out there.'

I was already familiar with this ceremony. Inside the long and slightly curved cigarillo was a dried blade of grass that served as a spill. When pulled out, it was used to light the cigar. My aunt will not countenance any mass-produced goods. Everything is handmade, even this straw mouthpiece.

'You can stay outside and have some ice cream,' I said, 'and those who feel like it can carry on working.'

'Swot!' I heard Fanny say. Intellectual curiosity isn't her strong suit. Fabian, however, was hooked on Aunt Fé's stories about money; he simply couldn't get enough.

1 J. W. von Goethe, *Faust, Part Two* (David Luke trans. and introd.) (Oxford: Oxford University Press, 1994).

'Very well,' she said. 'If you really are keen. Banknotes were far from the final word. More and more new pieces of paper came out over time. Bills of exchange, notices of credit and cheques. Some were even known as "participation certificates". Shares were printed in increasing quantities too, beautifully illustrated, absolutely magnificent. One could put them in the safe or hang them on the wall. They used to have accoutrements—coupons—which could be cut off with small pair of scissors. If all went well, shareholders would receive cash in hand every year without lifting a finger. Those were called "payouts" or "dividends". Carl von Fürstenberg, a famous banker back in the good old days, did not mince his words: "Shareholders are stupid and impertinent: stupid because they buy shares, and impertinent because they demand dividends." He knew what would happen when the company issuing the documents got into trouble. Those slips of paper would be good for nothing but burning—they would go up in smoke.

'There was, however, another good thing about those securities: one could at least hold them in one's hands. Now they are invisible, merely a number in a warehouse to which the owner has no access. But one doesn't have to immediately go out and found a stock company. How about a limited company or a joint-stock company? The advantage is that you are not liable with all your assets.'

'I want to go home. It's too hot here.' This was Fanny's only comment.

'We can turn the air conditioning on again. I can't work it properly—there are so many buttons. But Fabian

knows how to work the thing. What are you drinking, Fanny?'

'Sprite,' she replied. She'd come in from the balcony because she was curious to know what we were discussing.

'Bad for your teeth! A disgusting beverage. But money can take the same form: it's called liquidity.'

'Another of your foreign words!'

'Get used to it, my dears! Economics can't exist without a little strange vocabulary. Being liquid means you're solvent, and that in turn means that you can pay. If you aren't solvent, you're bankrupt. They pull the chairs from under your bottoms. Only if you're not a major bank, though—then you're too big to fail.'

'More jargon,' Fabian objected. The few lines from *Faust* had been lost on him too. He preferred instruction manuals and car magazines to literature.

'Imagine setting out to build the tallest possible house of cards. That's roughly the way the financial system works. The cards at the bottom are key. Take one away and the whole structure could come crashing down. It's everyone's nightmare. So a bank that holds one of those cards has nothing to fear: it must be saved at all costs. If disaster strikes, it receives a cash injection from the central bank or the state, and the taxpayers picks up the tab.

'Empty your pockets and you'll see what your cash situation looks like. It can tinkle, flow, drip or dry up. But that's not the end of it—money can also evaporate completely. It vaporizes, turns into a gas and forms bubbles.

You can no longer take it in hand. It's similar to inflation. Do you know what that means? Inflation comes from the word "*flatus*". That's Latin!'

'Stop!' Fanny cried. 'We're supposed to learn Latin now?'

'Children, my Latin doesn't stretch much farther than that, but I do recall what "flatus" means. Something like "fart". It crops up in a notorious Roman classic. The emperor at the time was Vespasian, who is said to have invented the urinal. He wanted to fill the state's coffers with the proceeds from public conveniences. He would probably have been forgotten long ago if he hadn't gone down in history for a nifty little slogan: "Money does not stink." '

'You've got to have some first,' Fabian interjected.

'I once questioned a cashier about it. He spent all day counting money—his hands were so dirty after work that he had to scrub them with soap. His job was merely to count deposits and withdrawals in a branch office. People at headquarters no longer need to touch big sums because money is completely invisible now, like a ghost or a phantom. There's no metal any more, no paper, no liquid, no gas—nothing but rows and rows of ones and zeroes on a screen. Completely digital, like the chip on this credit card.'

She was in full flow again. 'In America,' she complained, 'people get very suspicious if you try to pay for something with cash. Cash laughs, my uncle always said, but that was a long time ago. Anyone who has a say, bankers and economists, would like to abolish cash as soon as possible. Why? You have three guesses. So they can better control what we do and what we don't do.'

By now we were sprawling in our armchairs and had had enough of her explanations.

'Oh, you're starting to yawn,' Aunt Fé said, waving her stick at us. 'If you're bored, we'll do something different. What do you fancy? Have you ever been to a prison? Or would you prefer to sit in on a court case? I could ring up an old acquaintance of mine who's a barrister.'

'I'd rather not.'

'Doesn't one of you have an idea?'

It was Fabian who raised his hand. 'I went to an auction a few months ago. You should experience one too. It's more fun than a court trial between neighbours fighting over a fence or a plum tree.'

He'd never mentioned this before. Aunt Fé wanted to hear all about it.

'You'd never imagine the kind of thing people leave behind. Not just umbrellas and hats, but watches, clothes and suitcases with their entire contents too. A few times a year, the airport auctions off a huge quantity of items from Lost and Found. It's amazingly cheap! My new phone, for example. I only paid 40 euros for it. It costs 10 times that much in a shop.'

'Where is it held?'

'They put up a marquee at a village fête somewhere. The auctioneer, who looks like a livestock dealer, starts the bidding at 5 euros. Who's ready to up their offer? One man bought a walking stick and a pair of binoculars for 20 euros; another bid twice that much for a chainsaw. Once, a wedding dress went on sale. They don't accept cheques or credit cards, though. It's cash only.'

Aunt Fé praised his enthusiasm and yet couldn't resist trumping him. 'Next time, if you like, we'll go to an art auction. At a very famous establishment, right here in town. They sent me a catalogue of Old Masters. Now, where did I put it? I believe the auction is next Wednesday. But that's enough for today. I'm worn out from all your chatter.'

Actually, she was the one who'd done most of the talking. Still, Fabian and I love our sessions with Aunt Fé. We have the scent of blood in our nostrils, so to speak. Not only do we pay more attention when our parents talk about their financial worries over dinner, we also stay to watch the late-night show on TV when someone pitches a rescue package or warns about the next euro crisis.

I've recently begun to grab the business section of the newspaper over breakfast. I find most crime novels more predictable than the stories those pages dish up on a daily basis. A murderer who commits a crime of passion is pretty innocent compared with your run-of-the-mill white-collar criminal. You rub your hands in glee reading about another hedge-fund manager who has fetched up behind bars, even though you know he'll soon be out again for good behaviour and his successor will only carry on with the same shady business. I found no less than four striking articles in yesterday's issue of the *Frankfurter Allgemeine Zeitung*, the champion of German capitalism. The lead story began: 'Banks in Europe and America have been fined a hundred billion dollars for a number of fraudulent practices. Their crimes include violating economic sanctions and money-laundering laws, manipulating interest rates, abetting tax evasion, concealing risks, dubious mortgage lending and various other forms of deception.'

Yet the editors show no shortage of sympathy for an industry that's come under pressure. There has to be a fall guy, of course—even the whitest of flocks contains the occasional black sheep. Sadly, there's always the odd gentleman who throws himself out of a window, shoots himself or is found hanging from the underside of a bridge in London, but that's no reason to let a major bank go to the dogs. If that were to happen, where would it end?

My blood sometimes boils and I rage against the class bias of our legal system, a nineteenth-century notion I picked up from left-wing groups. Little Fanny covers her ears with her hands when I raise such arguments. At least I can discuss this kind of thing with Fabian. The economic jargon does get on his nerves, though. He thinks the analysts and investment advisers are all charlatans, acting like big shots in order to pocket huge salaries and commissions. If they came up with even one nailed-on tip, they'd be richer than any of their employers or clients.

My mother doesn't understand why we're interested in these things. 'It's enough for people like us to make ends meet. It's a waste of time, what you're doing!' She doesn't trust our aunt as far as she could throw her. 'Fé's craftier than you think,' she says. 'I honestly wonder what kind of games she's playing with you and what she tells you all day long. I hope you don't believe everything she says.'

'You think she's lying?'

'Not outright, no. But I hope you won't fall for her airs and graces. After all, you do know about some of her escapades.'

Once again Herr Forster pulled up punctually at half past ten in his limousine. How come he was always ready at whenever Aunt Fé needed him? He was supposed to be at the other guests' disposal too. How did she manage to have him serve as her private chauffeur? I didn't get it.

Fanny didn't come with us this time.

'Enough special outings for you, little lady. You're going to school,' Mum decided. She was right too, because Fanny wouldn't have been allowed into the art auction. All buyers must be over eighteen and register in a sort of guest book. Only then are they given a cardboard badge with a bidder number on it. Fabian was able to sneak in because he was so tall and because he had altered his student card with indelible pencil.

The proceedings in the hall were totally different from his description of the lost-and-found auction. The auctioneer was an English-looking gentleman dressed in black with a white gardenia in his buttonhole; his entrance was worthy of a celebrity conductor. Most of the attendees seemed to know one another, and were nodding and whispering. Some of the ladies wore wide-brimmed hats. Fabian felt out of place in his T-shirt and jeans, but Aunt Fé pointed to a billionaire in the row in front of him, dressed like a tramp. 'The man next to him is a curator from a museum in California, and those men in a huddle at the back are London art dealers.'

Silence fell as the auctioneer took to his lectern and gave a short, witty welcome speech. A female assistant kept an eye on the phone. Two underlings wearing white gloves carried in the first painting. Lot Number One! They never start with the most expensive pictures. I'd never heard of the artist, but the gentleman at the lectern praised him and provided some background about the work, its origins and its condition. The estimated price was printed in the catalogue, which everyone had studied well in advance. Some of the bidders weren't even present: they had sent in offers in writing or were represented by middlemen. Some secret buyers were also following the bidding by phone.

After a while, two assistants rolled in the 'star lot': an oversized sheepdog made of pink Plexiglas. Its ears were gilded, and it had a small plaster Madonna in its mouth.

The whole thing struck me as one of those performances where the director stands up on stage while the actors are scattered around the theatre. The only genuine spectators were insignificant people like us. We were able to follow the bids on a big screen as they rose in increments of a thousand. The prices were displayed in euros, pounds and dollars.

I watched the auctioneer admiringly as he bobbed and weaved behind his lectern, raising the temperature in the room with each successive phone bid. Despite delivering his furious patter, not a single gesture in the room escaped his attention. Some people didn't even bother to raise their badge. A twitch of a finger or a raised eyebrow was enough to add a few thousand to the price.

The bidding wars were the best. Fabian and I watched breathlessly as two rutting stags goaded each other on. Did they have some information that had escaped everyone else's attention?

'Fair warning!' called the auctioneer, indicating that this was people's last chance to make an offer. The frantic contest ended at 8.5 million. One of the two opponents threw in the towel and the hammer came down. This was followed by a string of failures, however. A numb silence fell over the room, signalling a run of losses. 'Unsold,' the gentleman at the lectern mumbled before moving on to the next lot.

And Aunt Fé? Her eyes roamed around the room as if she were in a museum. She had no intention of making a purchase.

'Wasn't that an entertaining morning?' she asked us over lunch in the hotel conservatory.

'Why didn't you bid?' I asked her in return. 'Some of those items were really tempting.'

'I used to collect anything and everything, but that's all over now. I don't need any more clutter.'

'I enjoyed myself. The other attendants seemed unbelievably smug, but I was impressed by how calmly the business was conducted. Every object is announced "as is", meaning that the buyer has to keep his eyes open. No one is favoured or fooled.'

'Do you agree, Fabian?' said Aunt Fé, adopting her most malicious smile. 'What about the holes?'

'What do you mean?'

'Oh, my dears, the art trade is like a Swiss cheese. Shot through with cavities. You know what they call it? Discretion!'

Fabian wanted to know more.

'I prefer not to mention the hefty premiums added to the bill at the end, the guarantees and the stooges. Nor do I wish to bore you with the peculiar attributions, the biased reports, the miraculous restorations and touching-up. There's something more fascinating than any of those little tricks—the cartels.'

'There's no one listening in, Aunt Fé. You don't have to speak in riddles.'

'There's no need to pretend to be more stupid than you really are, Fabian. Cartels are very common, and not only in the elevated spheres of the art world. It doesn't matter if it's coffee beans, railway tracks or cement: wherever there's competition—and let's face it, where isn't there?—you'll always find a few gentlemen gathered in a back room. And they *are* usually men, of course. Suitable hotels are ten a penny, and the expenses can be set off against tax. In those rooms they agree on pricing and divide up the markets to avoid treading on one another's toes. The same shenanigans go on in large construction projects with large sums of money at stake. Airports or concert halls, for example. They are subject to public calls for tender. Undermining competition is against the law, of course. There are monopolies commissions in place to prevent it, but they have a tough job on their hands.'

'They never really manage to crack down on it,' Fabian declared.

'How can they? The mafia have good lawyers too. Incidentally, these things are generally dealt with in a very genteel fashion. "Messy situations" are avoided and business settled without bloodshed. Occasionally a cartel is dismantled because one of the participants comes clean. He turns state's evidence, gets off scot-free, and the others pay a fine out of their petty cash, which is always preferable to jail.'

'How depressing.'

'I agree! But, if nothing else, our little outing has given you a glimpse into the world of art history *and* taught you something about the "national" economy, which most of the nation doesn't understand. Now, perhaps we should have a semifreddo for dessert. Maybe coconut or elderflower flavour—what do you think? After that I need my siesta.'

As we said goodbye, another thought crossed her mind.

'I've lost track of things. One becomes forgetful at my age. We've never discussed the difference between money and capital. We must rectify that next time you come.'

Once again, our mother interrogated us. 'So what did you talk about today?'

Yet when I attempted to explain how an auction works and how a cartel operates, she didn't want to listen.

'Have you found out why she keeps coming? She must have her reasons. Maybe she has business to take care of or meetings with important people. I find it hard to believe she comes purely to visit relatives.'

'Maybe she just likes us.'

'All of this just to impress you with her luxury hotel and her dubious outings? That isn't at all Fé's style.'

I had to agree with my mother there. I didn't think our aunt capable of spending hours on the train out of the goodness of her heart. I decided to get to the bottom of the matter.

Fanny was allowed to come to our next session, as she was off school that particular Wednesday. She had got out of her singing lesson because she was apparently neither willing nor able to sing, even though she was musical and usually loved to perform in public. These abilities had attracted the attention of a jaunty supply teacher who wanted to teach her the flute, although he charged her for the pleasure, unfortunately.

'Why don't you ask Aunt Fé whether she'd pay for it,' our father suggested. This was an additional reason for taking Fanny along.

Everything was as usual, apart from the fact that we found our aunt sitting with a turban on her head and a girl in a white coat crouching at her feet. 'I'm having my pedicure. We've almost finished,' she said. 'Make yourselves at home.'

She'd obviously forgotten what she'd been planning to teach us. Sometimes our aunt harps on about a subject, and at others just jumbles together a variety of topics. Taking a systematic approach isn't her strong suit. I thought it might be best to jog her memory.

'You wanted to explain the difference between money and capital.'

'Oh, is that all? That's easy. Show me the contents of your pockets.'

There wasn't much in them.

'I always run out of money straight away.'

'Because you're not careful, Fanny.'

'It's better to spend it fast.'

'You may be right. That way you don't need to worry about where to put it. Capital is what you have left over.'

'You can hide it under the mattress like Bozena, or in a piggy bank if you have one.'

'Obviously *you* won't be so stupid, because you've realized that money has to work.'

'Work?'

'Of course. That means that it mustn't be left lying around. It needs investing. Then it's no longer money but capital. Birds of a feather flock together. You just have to scrape together enough to get started. If you're lucky and know the ropes, capital breeds more capital. You know what money does? Money makes more money! It's called accumulation.'

'Because you receive interest on your capital, and compound interest on your interest.' Fabian again, who owed this wisdom to the woman at the building society.

'Quite so. But it depends on the interest rate. Most children have percentage calculations drummed into them in primary school, but as soon as they've put that tedium behind them, they'd rather never hear another word about it. Which is unfortunate.'

'I could gladly do without all that fiddly arithmetic.'

'As you please, Fanny. But the other two will know how long it takes for a number to double if it grows at 7 per cent per year?'

'What kind of number do you mean?'

'Any number. It doesn't matter if it is related to economic growth, capital, prices, rents or population growth. At 7 per cent, anything and everything doubles in 10 years. That's basic maths.'

'And it goes on like that for ever and ever?'

'If only! Unfortunately—or thank God—that is impossible. One day, growth slows, interest starts to fall and the dream is over. The numbers decline and everything dwindles as quickly as it increased. After 10 years of 7 per cent inflation, your money is worth only half as much as before. And when the interest rate is falling, as it is now, you can say goodbye to any kind of yield on your savings account.' Aunt Fé laughed sardonically. 'A small saver used to be able to simply lie back and wait. Nowadays, though, people will laugh at you if you keep all your pennies naively in one pot. So much for your pension! You'll have been slowly and truly fleeced by the time you grow old. That's why the general advice is to invest in material assets, my dears. Land, stocks, shares, venture capital—those are the watchwords in times like these. Of course, whether you like it or not, that makes you a speculator.'

Maybe we shouldn't have brought Fanny along because instead of listening attentively, like her brother, she chewed sullenly on her cinnamon-flavoured gum. All she said was, 'Do whatever you want with your capital, but leave me in peace.'

'Fine, Fanny. If you've no wish to be rich, then you can forget about such tedious matters. It has its advantages, though. No need to get upset if you fall flat on your face because the share price collapsed, because there are empty stores in your shopping centre or because your PLC has cancelled its dividends. Or your asset manager has just run off to the Caribbean with your valuable portfolio.

'But anyone who doesn't take your stance, Fanny, needs to deal with this business, and by that I mean especially you, Fabian. They don't teach this in high school. If you like, I'll tell you about the constant cycle of ups and downs. Boom and bust. No one really knows what lies behind it, and it's not as if famous theorists haven't tried their best. Gentlemen like Adam Smith, Max Weber, Schumpeter, Keynes and Hayek and a few dozen others. One of their finest inventions was the economic cycle, by which they mean something like the alternation of high and low tides. They simply would not accept that such anonymous gods as chance and randomness governed the economy. Their research didn't lead them much further than that. The only thing that is clear is that crises are not an exception—they're the rule. They're part and parcel of the mechanics of capitalism. Upturn, overheating, stagnation, recession, collapse. Nor are the recipes for cranking up the economy new.'

Fabian was knowledgeable about cars, and at this punchline, his patience finally snapped. 'Why do capitalists always talk as if the economy were a 1920s Oldsmobile? Back then, when the engine stalled, you got out the crank handle, stuck it through the cooler into the flywheel and gave it a few good twists. Step on the gas, drive off, put your foot to the floor and the economic miracle's off and running!'

'You're right, Fabian! The economy is not an old car. It's probably more like a casino. Everyone around the table imagines that sooner or later he or she will make a killing. Some people eagerly study company financial statements while others hire mathematicians because they think they'll be able to supply precise forecasts. Or they have a friend who slips them cast-iron insider tips. You won't believe this, but two of the billionaires I've met regularly consult a fortune-teller or an astrologist.'

'Knowing you, Aunt Fé, I'd guess you were into that too.'

'I used to be, yes.'

'So you were superstitious?'

'There's nothing unusual about that. Don't you ever take an umbrella along because you think it's bound to rain? Your mother always knocks on wood when Franz claims nothing bad will happen to him again. He also believes that seven is his lucky number. How about you? You're probably too enlightened for such things, my dear.'

'I visited our cousin in New York once. Her name's Phillis. She sat at her computer every evening, checking the state of her portfolio. Her spirits rose when the stocks went up, and she was glum when they started to slide. There's no way I want that farce defining my mood— even if I were to come into a fortune one day.'

'So you're not interested in private equity? How about convertible or zero bonds?'

'Oh cut it out, Aunt Fé!'

'If you only knew how often *I*'ve fallen flat on *my* face . . .'

'What happened?'

'Leveraged options! Bets on bets, you could call them.'

'It serves you right, Aunt Fé!' Fanny'd had enough of this conversation and could contain herself no longer. I dragged her off the couch where she was lounging, apologized to Aunt Fé and threatened to take the little whinger home, even though both Fabian and I were desperate to find out more about the stock market.

Luckily, Fanny calmed down, allowing our aunt to continue: 'The only things they've never been able to lure me into are the airplane game and the pyramid scam. Both work like a chain letter, and the last people in are always the ones who lose out. I've never trusted derivatives either—they're the financial industry's weapons of mass destruction, packages whose contents it is impossible to know. Inside each box are always more boxes, and the final box usually turns out to be empty.'

By now all three of us were exhausted, so we went home.

My father is a diehard sceptic, and even less of a fan of the capital markets than Aunt Fé is. That might not always have been the case, though. I think he probably blew some of the little money he had as a young man. He once confessed to me that a friend had persuaded him

to 'go for dollars'. That must have been back in the early 80s. He didn't stake much, but he's shied away from similar gambles since. He has never complained. If he loses something, he greets the setback with sarcasm. My accounts of Aunt Fé's lessons reminded him of a hit song from the days of the economic miracle: 'Konjunktur', or 'Boom and Bust'. He hummed the tune to me, but he'd forgotten the words.

I couldn't get this golden oldie out of my head, so I looked it up online. It was apparently a massive hit back in the 60s, and everyone in my father's generation knew the Hazy Osterwald Sextett number off by heart. The lyrics go: '*Gehn Sie mit, gehn Sie mit, mit der Konjunktur / gehn Sie mit, gehn Sie mit auf diese Tour!*'—'Ride along, ride along with boom and bust / ride along, oh yes you must!' It made me laugh so much that I sang it to Fanny over breakfast.

For days Fanny had been fussing about her seventh birthday. Such was the grandeur of the occasion that she regarded the Federmann's humble abode as an unsuitable location for the celebrations. She was intent on going to the Four Seasons.

'How do you intend to go about this? Are you planning to invite your whole gang?' Mum asked her. 'I can't imagine your aunt agreeing to that.'

Mum was absolutely right. Well in advance, Aunt Fé informed Fanny, 'You are welcome, as always, and I don't mind if you bring *one* of your best friends with you.'

'Well, we'll celebrate twice then,' Fanny said and stuck to this plan even when Mother pointed out that her meagre household allowance left no margin for the kind of extravagances Fanny was dreaming of. The whole family sighed and we had to buy presents for her, disfigure the rooms with colourful garlands and use the largest saucepan we owned to cook for all her classmates.

I'd rather not recall Fanny's twittering and screeching friends. On the evening after her party, she sat in a sea of wrapping paper and fell into a long brooding silence. The object of these ruminations was to come to a strategic decision as to which lucky girl she should introduce to Aunt Fé. The winner was a certain Linda, a flaxen-haired, taciturn creature whose main advantage was that she could be guaranteed not to outshine our Fanny.

The meeting at the Four Seasons proved a triumph for the birthday girl. Yet again she had got her way. When Herr Forster picked us up, a small welcome bouquet stood in an old-fashioned vase on the dashboard. Room service at the hotel surpassed itself. No comparison with the hotdogs and potato salad at home! After congratulations had been proffered, there was a toast to Fanny's health, and Aunt Fé presented her with a black case engraved with her initials, FF. On the velvet lining lay a gleaming silver flute. I found the whole thing well over the top, given the sounds my sister was capable of producing on the recorder.

Next, little Linda launched into a rendition of 'Happy Birthday'. Her solo was so crystal-clear that we all fell silent and then broke into applause at the end. Fanny was not to be outdone. Although she supposedly cannot sing, she began to warble the old hit I'd taught her: '*Gehn Sie mit, gehn Sie mit, mit der Konjunktur / gehn Sie mit, gehn Sie mit auf diese Tour!*'

These lines obviously reminded Aunt Fé of old times, and she was visibly impressed and pleased by Fanny's performance. 'I've looked up your birthday, my dear Fanny, and observed that you were born under a lucky star. Also, you are a twin.'

'Huh? No one ever told me that!'

'Your star sign. Gemini. 11 June 2006 at exactly half past two in the afternoon. Do you know what that means?'

'She's in shock, Aunt Fé,' I said and to put Fanny's mind at rest, I whispered in her ear, 'Astrology, that's all.'

'Jupiter in the Second House of your birth chart is a sign of future success, my child, and you'll never lack for money because you have Mercury in the Tenth.'

'That's nonsense,' I cried.

'I had a horoscope done for her, and Mars in Leo shows that she is a princess.'

'Or would like to be.'

'Neptune in the Fifth may mean that she'll pursue an artistic career.'

'We know what she's like. She just wants to show off!'

Fanny was beaming at our aunt's announcements.

'You've no idea what her bedroom looks like!' we cried in unison.

'I can easily imagine. Messy! And I'm willing to bet that she's always late. She's insolent at school. I can tell from her Mars that she tends to be impatient, but we won't hold that against her.'

'Do you really believe in this stuff, Aunt Fé?'

'Oh no! It's merely a game, a pastime, like the lottery or the financial markets. There too, some people have all the luck while others are jinxed, and since no one knows which they are, they cling to their soothsayer, an old gypsy woman or some nerd tossing out mathematical formulas. Anyway, astrologists are like tinkers, always arguing. This acquaintance of mine who did Fanny's horoscope rips his colleagues to shreds. But I notice that your eyelids are drooping, birthday girl, and I imagine that your little friend Linda isn't up to an encore.'

Unaware of the future ups and downs of which the horoscope made no mention, we bade our aunt a polite goodbye. Fanny even gave a curtsey of delight at the prospect of taking her prized flute home with her.

That midsummer we were trapped in our daily routine again. Aunt Fé had disappeared from our lives as suddenly as she had entered it. No farewell message. No note to the three of us. No explanation . . . We all missed her, even our mother who had been so critical of her. Fanny was sulking because no one had taken any notice of her since her birthday extravaganza, and because the smart flute teacher was so impressed by her pricey instrument that he was threatening her with extra lessons.

I should have known better. After all, I knew my godmother well enough to recognize her moods and whims. I had often wondered why she came to our city. She had never volunteered any reason for her trips. Nine weeks in a hotel simply to haunt the Federmanns? That wasn't her style at all. So I tried to figure out her secret. I sent a brief and cautious message to her villa on the shores of Lake Geneva. No reply!

There was nothing to be done. I didn't fancy ringing La Pervenche. In any case, I would most likely only have got through to her housekeeper or butler.

'Maybe she's travelling again,' my father said, 'or else she simply doesn't wish to be disturbed.'

I decided to concentrate on my tedious A-levels rather than yearn for those wonderful, lost afternoons at the Four Seasons.

If you have the time and inclination, come to see me at the hotel next Wednesday afternoon.

II

THE RETURN OF AUNT FÉ

If her disappearance had been unexpected, so was the arrival of her message two months later. This time it was a colourized postcard from Lisbon.

If you have the time and the inclination, come to see me at the hotel next Wednesday afternoon read the scrawl, as always in green ink. The photo was of an empty square with a wave-patterned mosaic. The caption said 'Praça de Dom Pedro'. I immediately looked it up online. Dom Pedro was King of Portugal and Emperor of Brazil. Again, I was at a loss as to how my beloved aunt had fetched up in Lisbon.

She didn't waste much breath explaining why she'd forsaken us for so many weeks. She also ignored Fanny's request for a sundae. She began instead with a question to which none of us had a ready answer.

'My dears, tell me what you intend to do with your lives!'

Fabian piped up first, stammering slightly. 'I think my greatest wish is to be rich.'

'To what end, Fabian?'

'I know the answer to that. Because the worse the pay, the more tedious and horrible the work. It simply isn't true that money stinks. In fact, the opposite is true— it's always the poor who live in dirty, loud, crowded and toxic conditions. I can't begin to imagine how people in a slum get by on a dollar a day. Probably by working illegally or sending their children out to beg. On the other hand, the more comfortable, cushy and pleasant the work is, the more you earn. Gentlemen sitting around in their executive chairs in nice, warm rooms with secretaries bringing them coffee. And when they're away on business, they take a suite at the Four Seasons, like you. That's why I'm determined not to be poor.'

We were all struck by Fabian's candour. Aunt Fé smiled but refrained from any comment.

'And you, Felicitas? What are your plans? I'm sure you're ambitious!'

'Oh yeah!' Fanny blurted out. 'Everyone at her school says she's a total swot. Always going on about exams! Disturb her when she's revising and she bites your head off. And you know what she talks about, Aunt Fé? Her average grade. Do you know what that is?'

'No. I believe I failed a few exams at your age. My father was forced to send me to a Catholic boarding school, an incredibly expensive one. Sister Anselma always cheated a little to balance the books—the parents were ready to riot over a bad school report. All for a scrap of paper everyone soon forgot. It's unbelievable how seriously people take exams. Bachelor, Master of Something-or-Other, PhD . . . I hold such things in low esteem. The Americans are far more easy-going. They give you a chance, wherever you come from, and a company will only sack you if you turn out to be hopeless. Don't mind me, though, Felicitas. If your heart is set on it, do as you see fit and study for a doctorate somewhere.'

'That's not the point. I'm not doing it for the title.'

'What do you want to be?'

'That's simple: I never want to have a boss telling me what to do. Nor a working day that lasts from nine to half past five, nor unpaid overtime as a test of my resilience. There's no way I'm going to apply to a bank or an insurance company that coops up its employees in open-space cages.'

'It is unfortunate that they abandoned those magnificent palaces with servants in livery to greet you on the steps!'

'My motto is: Less money, more independence. That's the most important thing.'

'I see. You mean self-employed. Freelancing always *sounds* so appealing.'

'Time is money—one of those stupid sayings. The opposite is just as true, though: you can buy time with money. Which is why I say yes to work, but only where and when I feel like it.'

'I see. Like artists, architects, pettifoggers, actors, tennis players and so on. I do fear, though, that most freelancers delude themselves into believing that they are freer than their peers. It's quite a risky business. I suspect that their ranks are teeming with starvelings.'

'I know. But what about you? You've always managed to preserve your independence.'

'Always? How would you know? My situation hasn't always been as good. I can tell you about the old days another time, though, if you'd like me to. Not today. The others have spoken, Fanny, but you've been silent. What is *your* goal?'

'Adults always ask me that. "What do you want to be when you grow up?" It starts in your first year at school. Dad's the only one who never mentions it, though he's probably worried too. Why should I think about it so early? Can't you just leave me in peace?'

'What would you do if you had money?'

'Money is round, so it rolls away on its own. Which is what makes it so easy to spend. It's gone before you've even had time to think what you're going to do with it.'

'That's a good point,' said Aunt Fé, frowning, and I thought I glimpsed a rueful glimmer in her violet eyes. It only lasted for a split second, though, and then she was back on the attack. 'Why are the three of you just sitting there? It'd be better if you came up with some ideas of your own. I'm not your schoolteacher. No one's paying me to keep you on your toes.'

Fanny raised her hand and said, 'I've got something.'

'At long last.'

'The inside of the lift is covered with pictures of a swimming pool. Why don't we go there? What are "spa", "peeling" and "wellness", and where is it?'

'I don't know, Fanny. The pool may be in the basement. We can ask at Reception.'

'No, it must be right at the top. There're a lot of big windows on the pictures.'

'Then it's out on the roof. If you really are keen, we can go and have a look. Fanny, "wellness" means feeling good.'

We took the lift up to the top floor. A sign said, 'Children are welcome from 10 a.m. to 4 p.m.'

'It's almost four now. They won't let me in,' Fanny objected.

'We'll see about that. Who is in charge here? You?'

'Absolutely no problem, madam,' said a man whose white coat and pointed moustache made him look like a cross between a lifeguard and a waiter. 'Bathrobes, swimming costumes and towels are down there on the left.'

Fanny was over the moon. The pool was bigger than I'd imagined. There was a bar. There were deckchairs everywhere with fabulous views of the city's towers and rooftops. I picked up one of the menus and studied what was on offer: Thai massage, ayurveda, steam baths, yoga, peeling, face masks, the lot.

'Everything a woman could want,' I said under my breath.

'Oh no, there's pampering for men too,' our aunt remarked, glancing over my shoulder. 'Energy shower gel! Anti-ageing! One big con, if you ask me. And what's that I see down there? Those ugly machines, on which people with nothing better to do can pedal away like mad. There are even "workouts" for people to recover from the chronic stress of their useless occupations.'

'You have to have money to get in,' said Fanny.

'There's no doubt about that. Rich people like to be with other rich people.'

'There are some American cities where they've locked themselves into neighbourhoods you need a special pass to enter.'

'Do you know any genuinely rich people, Fabian?'

'Only from the newspaper and TV. And there are a few up here too.'

'I don't care. I'm going for a swim,' said Fanny. 'Who's coming with me?'

Fanny was the best swimmer in our family. She dived headfirst into the pool and demonstrated how long she could stay underwater.

'Are you coming in, Aunt Fé?'

'I was always too lazy to learn to swim properly. I'd rather watch. Why are you so curious about the rich? Nobody likes them, but everyone wants to be like them. Their money's always been the most interesting thing about them, and they know it. Most of them are pretty boring, but one shouldn't tar them all with the same brush because they're just as diverse as the animals in a zoo. Some strut around like peacocks, while others are as shy as marmots and shun the limelight. There are lists showing how many zeroes they have to their names.'

'Those are the millionaires.'

'Oh, that was long ago,' said my aunt. 'Nowadays, there are millions of millionaires wherever you look. The club includes anyone who owns a thriving butcher's shop or a flat in the right part of town—it's getting a little crowded in there. No. Nine zeroes are the minimum to be considered properly rich.'

'You mean they need a billion.'

'At least. An annual list of the members of the club is published in America, and it gets longer every year. But no one seems to care about a zero here or there any more. The national debt smashed through the trillion barrier without politicians even batting an eyelid. Ordinary people can't get their heads around those kinds of figures anyway. And to confuse them further, some countries refer to our billions as trillions!'

'I don't want to hear any more about it.'

'Fair enough, Fabian.'

'But do you know any billionaires or whatever they're called?'

'A couple once invited me to the Algarve. That's in Portugal. They owned a large house next to a golf course. One day, they received a surprise visit from an American family. Distant acquaintances. Bankers or managers or something—the man of the house knew them from a company's board of directors. They were trying to tick off every exclusive golf club in Europe during their holidays, and that's what'd brought them to my hosts' door.'

'Why are you telling us this?'

'Because after they left, the lady of the house turned to me and said, "What tactful people! Not once did they make us feel like poor devils because my husband is only worth a few tens of millions."'

'How horrid.'

'Oh, they were really very nice. There's far worse. Some filthy rich people are incredible misers. Once I was in Paris when an arms dealer invited 70 people to dine at the most expensive restaurant in the city. He cut and ran after dessert, leaving his guests to settle the bill.'

'Anyone who accepts an invitation from a man like that gets exactly what they deserve.'

'Does the name Getty ring any bells? He was an American oil tycoon and billionaire. I never met him, but he was famous for his peculiar behaviour. A group of Italian gangsters abducted his grandson when he was about your age, Fabian. The kidnappers demanded a ransom of 17 million dollars in exchange for his release. His grandfather refused to pay. It was only when the extortionists cut off the boy's ear and posted it to a newspaper in Rome that he sent them a first instalment. I don't remember how it was all resolved, but at least the boy survived. His grandfather bought a huge sixteenth-century castle in southern England. You've not heard the famous anecdote about the telephone? The billionaire was annoyed that his guests were constantly ringing their wives and friends all over the world and costing him a fortune. So he purchased one of those small red phone boxes, and from then on the guests always had to have a few shillings on hand if they wanted to call someone.'

'What a cheapskate!'

'Yes, but that's only one side of the story. That self-same Getty was also a fantastic patron of the arts and philanthropist. He founded a famous museum, with free entry for all, containing thousands of paintings, sculptures, drawings and manuscripts, a research centre and lots of other facilities.'

'Like Warren Buffett and Bill Gates.'

'Old money and new money. Some people set great store by that distinction. The old consider themselves superior and look down on the new, call them *parvenus*.'

'Oh please, Aunt Fé!'

'Upstarts, newly wealthy, social climbers. As if those were insults! Such nonsense. Even princes started out small, as land-enclosers and robber barons, and so did the Rothschilds, the railroad tycoons, the Carnegies and the Krupps. They're all the same! One used to be able to tell who belonged to the upper crust. I'm old enough to have heard chatter about "high society". Nowadays, there are only celebrities—people you see on television and in the tabloid press. Footballers, counts selling cars in China, popstars, housewives who've written a bestseller, and last but not least the talk-masters!'

'I've never heard that word before.'

'That's what they call themselves in Germany because they like to sound American. Talk-show hosts. Their sort used to perform in music halls and be part of bohemian society.'

'You don't like them?'

'I think I was a spoilt tearaway myself when I was young.'

'What I don't get about the super-rich, Aunt Fé, is this: if someone has more money than he knows what to do with, then why can't he give up profiteering? Just to own an even bigger yacht than everyone else?'

'It depends entirely on whom you're comparing yourself with. Have you ever heard of marginal benefit?'

'Don't think so.'

'It's simple, really. The more millions you have, the lower the benefit of earning an extra hundred. A millionaire once told me an anecdote when I asked him what drove him to keep accumulating money: a philanthropist tosses a 200-euro note onto a homeless man's metal plate. The homeless man is stunned and overjoyed. His benefactor says to himself, "This man is happy with so little! It would take a successful merger with my Australian competitor to make me as euphoric as he is."

'That gentleman told me that he didn't care about petty cash. The example shows that being rich isn't simply a pursuit—it's a kind of profession. Most of those people would have trouble giving it up, and even if one of the super-rich were to forget about his billions, his peers would be sure to remind him.'

'I'm perfectly happy when you slip me a tenner or two, Aunt Fé. I'll be able to afford a new bike one day.'

'So remember marginal benefit. You don't require a university education to understand it.'

I was amazed to see how my brother and sister hung on Aunt Fé's every word. They'd never been this eager to learn at school. Even Fanny couldn't get enough.

'How can you tell how rich someone is?'

'I'll give you three guesses.'

'By their clothes.'

'If they drive a big car.'

'Or have a double garage.'

'They wear the smartest shoes.'

'It's easy to be fooled by details. Someone might walk into the lobby in jeans and a cheap T-shirt when actually he's buying up the hotel. Or the other way around: the guy in the immaculate white Brioni suit is an impostor who can't even afford his rent. See that Russian over there with the bulging pockets? He's going to pull out a bundle of 500-euro notes any moment now, but he might actually be on Interpol's wanted list. The only infallible guide is our concierge. Herr Stäuble has been honing his X-ray vision for decades. He knows the rules of the game—and he also knows how quickly they change.'

'What do you mean?'

'Think about it! In the past, the poor used to look half starved, and the wealthy, the princes, cardinals and other moneybags, were stout. Nowadays it's the opposite, especially in America. The worse the neighbourhood, the fatter its residents. And the same applies up here on the roof, especially for the women—nothing but skin and bone.'

'Even though you're one of them, you don't like the rich. You just won't admit it.'

'I've nothing against rich people, my dear Fabian! They're as inescapable as the weather. You can complain all you like about a rainy summer but it doesn't help a jot. Name me one human society that has managed to do away with this strange menagerie! The Bolsheviks tried at first, but their leaders were soon carving out comfortable lives for themselves. Lenin drove a Rolls-Royce, which you can now admire in a Moscow museum, and the revolutionaries moved into expropriated palaces. And, like wealth, poverty never disappears either.'

'That doesn't seem to bother you, Aunt Fé.'

'It depends what you mean by poverty, Fabian, and who has tinkered with the statistics. Do you mean absolute or relative poverty?'

'I'm sorry, but you're splitting hairs now. Everyone knows what it means to be poor.'

'I've no wish to bore you. Maybe you'd rather try out the sauna?'

'I'm too hot already.'

'Or a cold shower. They have broken ice for you to rub yourself down with.'

'You're just trying to change the subject.'

'Very well then, we'll stick to it. The World Bank says that anyone who has to live on less than 1 dollar per day is poor. Other institutions measure by the median, although I've forgotten precisely what that is. Some kind of average, I would guess. On the other hand, the World Health Organization, which is based in Rome, thinks that the poor are those who have less than 60 per cent of the average income in their pockets. As you can see, it's a tricky business.'

'How come?'

'Because it means that however prosperous a society, poverty is bound to increase. Imagine a country whose inhabitants have an average income of a million. Someone who earns only 500,000 would immediately be trapped in poverty. And everyone's afraid of that, even the proverbial little guy.'

'You're the only one who thinks he's so insignificant.'

'He's always scared. Of losing his precious job. Of his wife walking out, because divorce could ruin him. Of medical malpractice during a knee operation, leaving him in need of a wheelchair. He's haunted by the spectre of downward mobility.'

'You're probably in favour of illegal employment and against the minimum wage too.'

'You've got all worked up about that once before.'

I knew how this particular game of ping-pong would play out between my little brother and my aunt, the cunning cynic. Sooner or later Fabian would make a long speech about 'social justice'.

'It's a brilliant idea,' he declared.

'Only nothing's ever come of it. The fair society you picture has never been achieved. For thousands and thousands of years, every attempt to bring such a state into being, from Spartacus to Mao and Pol Pot, has ended in failure.'

'But the dream goes on.'

And so it continued. After claiming so recently and vociferously that he'd love to be rich, my brother of all people now clings to this utopia. Yet no one has been able to tell me in any detail what 'social justice'—a lazy catchphrase every party includes in its manifesto—would look like if anyone took it seriously. Nor could I stomach any more of Aunt Fé forcing my brother into a corner because she cannot stand his preaching. I would have done anything else, even a yoga course or a foot reflexology session, than have to listen to her endless prattle.

However, my aunt had yet another surprise up her sleeve—a eulogy for Karl Marx I would never have expected to hear from her.

'I once had a lover who was a dyed-in-the-wool Communist.' That was her opening gambit. 'In New York of all places. Greenwich Village, where I hung around in the early fifties. This handsome guy from the Midwest tried his best to teach me what the Party had to offer to people of my kind. He got nowhere with me, though. He tried to convert me with his leaflets, I opted to read *The Communist Manifesto* instead, and it taught me everything I needed to know.

'Now, Marx may have been a nasty piece of work, but he was not a phrasemonger and a fraud like his American comrades. Such an intelligent man, so incorruptible! Of course he never earned any serious money. He had to borrow from his friends to provide for his wife and children, and that upset him. He contracted a lot of painful boils and died from a lung tumour at 56. He was undoubtedly a hothead, but he analysed developments with the cold eye of a hawk, and that's rare. How I would have loved to have been able to chat with him!'

'What about?'

'A hundred and fifty years ago, he predicted that capitalism would come to a sticky end! I agree, I would have said to him, but when exactly? Surely not in our lifetimes?'

I can't tell you what she said after that because I resorted to my habitual excuse and claimed that I needed to revise for my ridiculous A-levels, unfortunately.

'I'm sorry, but you two can stay on if you like,' I said. 'I can make it home on my own.'

But they didn't fancy it either. Herr Forster was waiting at Reception to pick us up.

Later, back in my small bedroom, I fell to speculating once more. I wondered where my aunt really belonged. Left-wingers call this class analysis, I believe. Like my aunt, I've read the *Manifesto*—after all, it's only about 50 pages long. I had never studied the fat blue volumes, however. I did once specifically seek out *Capital* in the central library. Three books, over 2,500 pages. A patient librarian told me that Marx had never completed the bumper volume he intended as an explanation for everything. True believers say that you have to work your way through the *Theories of Surplus Value* which is just as thick. That's where I gave up, although I would have dearly loved to understand more.

It strikes me that our teachers and German newspaper editorialists never use the word 'class'. They prefer to talk about 'social categories', probably because they wanted nothing to do with Marxists.

People used to describe people like us, the Federmanns, as petty bourgeois. My father is definitely no proletarian, and Mum would never stand for being called working class.

In America and Britain, on the other hand, they still accept that class exists. Everyone there talks about upper, middle and lower class. If only that were the end of the matter! But no—people think it's important to cut the cake into the thinnest possible slices, which produces the upper-upper, the upper-middle, the middle-middle, the lower-middle, the upper-lower, the middle-lower and the lower-lower classes. It doesn't take a mathematician to figure out that you could go on and on until you had puff pastry.

You're getting nowhere, I tell myself, this is best left to sociologists. You'd do better to trust your nose; you don't need to read books for that. Most people—I would go so far as to say, virtually everyone—can immediately detect to which group a person belongs. It's hard to pin down what they base their opinion on. How someone talks, how they walk, what they eat, what they wear and where they live; a plethora of tiny clues. People have different levels of sensitivity. It's similar to the 'noses' of perfume makers, and coffee and tea tasters. Only a specialist like our concierge Herr Stäuble is able to gauge a guest's wealth, status and origins—in a word, his or her class—with a single glance, and if he so wished, he could even put his analysis into words. I haven't reached that stage yet, but I'm making progress.

I recently cottoned on to one of my aunt's secrets. I have no idea why the concierge is always so nice to me even though I've never tipped him. I enquired about a man who has caught my eye in the lift a couple of times and always gets out at my aunt's floor. He's extremely discreet, about 60 and always impeccably dressed with a casual pocket square and a white carnation in his buttonhole. He walks with a slight limp and speaks good English. He may well have studied at Oxford, but I pick up a hint of a German accent. I think he meets Aunt Fé each time she comes to town.

'That must be Herr Havelschmidt,' said Herr Stäuble.

'Who's he?'

'A very well-known Swiss lawyer who often stays here. His name occasionally appears in the newspaper, so I'm not giving away a secret, Fräulein Federmann.'

No Englishman alive has a name like Aunt Fé's visitor's. As far as I know, Havelschmidt isn't a Jewish name, but I'd bet a substantial sum that his family are émigrés.

Initially I considered whether he might be after Aunt Fé, as she's what is known as a 'good catch', but I doubt she's flirting with him. When I meet him in the lift, he's always carrying a briefcase with a combination lock. Does it have money inside? They negotiate, but I don't know the subject of their dealings. In any case, none of us is ever close enough to overhear anything when they withdraw to talk business.

The summer holidays arrived, putting an end to the lively sessions with Aunt Fé. Our parents were preparing for their holiday with no great excitement. They have a knack for finding cheap flights and inexpensive holiday cottages on Elba for the five of us. The sandy beach, the weekly market and the bus to Capoliveri were tediously familiar. Fabian and Fanny obviously had to go along, but I didn't feel like it.

'Holidays on Elba no longer good enough for you, eh?' my mother asked.

I once again used my A-level revision as a get-out-of-jail-free card and was allowed to stay at home, even though the exams were still a long way off.

My aunt didn't bear a grudge after I had run away from all the wellness, fitness and social justice of our last meeting. Quite the reverse, in fact. She very graciously invited me to the hotel lobby, emphasizing that it was for brunch rather than lunch. This was my chance to talk to her not *en famille* but in private for once.

'You don't walk enough,' I chided her. 'You only ever get Herr Forster to drive you around in the limousine! Why don't we go for a long walk, just the two of us? It's such a beautiful September day—cloudless and not too hot. And you'll be fine walking.'

'Quite right. I have no ailments to complain of, so far. Do you have any idea where we might go?'

'How about the Path of the Planets? It runs along the river and isn't too demanding.'

'And what does it have to do with the planets?'

'It passes nine boards showing details about the Sun's satellites: Mercury, Venus, the Earth, Mars, Jupiter, Saturn, Uranus, Neptune and Pluto.'

'You must have learnt those by rote at school.'

'No. I often go for a walk there. The clever part is that the planets not only pass you in the right order but at the right distance from the Sun. Every step along the path represents a million kilometres in space.'

'Am I going to make it?'

'The Path of the Planets isn't paved, which means it's easy on the feet. Do you fancy it? How about this afternoon?'

She couldn't resist this little adventure. I arranged for a taxi to take us to the starting point—the Sun. The central star was a gilded sphere that dominated the courtyard of a museum. In the first few strides we passed the boards representing Mercury and Venus. Soon we reached Earth. Thereafter the distances to the next wandering star began to lengthen.

As was her wont, my aunt was not minded to concentrate on astronomy. Before we had reached the next bridge, she asked me, 'Tell me, Felicitas, how do you feel about men? Do you have a steady boyfriend?'

'I've just dumped one.'

'He must have been scared of you. Most men panic when they meet a woman more intelligent than them.'

'Why are you so suspicious, Aunt Fé? It isn't healthy.'

'I may tell you another time. How far is it to Pluto?'

'A fair distance, over an hour. It's named after the god of the underworld. My Latin teacher claims that Pluto was the dispenser of wealth. Plato said that, apparently. It's possible that people worshipped him as a god, but he still had a dubious reputation. Some ancient Greeks accused him of being responsible for the hegemony of money.'

'Plutocracy.'

'You said it. The penniless in Athens were denied political rights. They weren't allowed to hold public office either. I don't think Aristotle was particularly enthusiastic about that regime.'

'My father Ferdinand had a similar experience. There was a three-class franchise system in Prussia at the time. The less taxes a man paid, the less say he had. That was the law until 1918. And you'll be aware, of course, that anyone dreaming of becoming the president of the US must be willing to fork out at least several billion on their campaign or they can forget it. I'll never understand why anyone would subject themselves to such torture.'

'It's getting a bit hot, Aunt Fé. There's a snack bar here. Do you fancy some iced tea?

'Will it be any good?'

'Hand me your stick and sit down on this bench.' I fetched two glasses of iced tea and sat down beside her. 'If you feel like it, I can tell you everything I've recently learnt about Pluto.'

'Go ahead. I'll gladly listen to what a greenhorn like you has tucked away inside her head, even though I do tend to forget most things young people say.'

'Astronomers looked for this planet for ages without success. Then, in 1930, a young American discovered it by chance. The grand old men of astronomy were deeply offended that a rookie had beaten them to the punch, while everyone else rejoiced at this addition to the night sky. A few years ago, however, Pluto was downgraded. So even an ancient god can see his star fade overnight.'

'It is the same with today's "global players", the "masters of the universe".'

'I guess you're not interested in hearing how a planet came to be demoted.'

'I am. This tea is out of a can and not very tasty, but it is doing me a power of good.'

'There was a huge argument at an astronomers' congress in Prague. At the end, there was a vote on whether Pluto should be demoted to a dwarf planet. The majority agreed that it should be, and so the old boy is now just one of a hundred thousand drifters in the solar system, with the same status as a comet or an asteroid.'

'So things have deteriorated so far in scientific circles that a majority vote can decide the truth, have they? All very democratic, like parliament.'

'I pity old Pluto.'

'Life isn't all tragic, child. One must see the funny side too. In matters of the heart, for example.'

'All right, we'll forget about the stars and keep our feet firmly on the ground instead. How many times have you been married, Aunt Fé?'

'Two and a half times, I believe.'

'Was the "half" a common-law marriage? Concubinage—isn't that what they used to call it?'

'It was such a long, long time ago.'

'Even better.'

'My first husband was an irresistible Latin Lothario, an Argentinian. He came from a good family but he was utterly unscrupulous. Picture a man of 22, quite a dandy, trilingual and an outstanding tango dancer. I was studying in Vassar—a women-only college at the time. A fairly extortionate place. A magnificent campus in a dump called Poughkeepsie on the Hudson River. Handsome Antonio lived with his parents in a nearby town called

Rhinebeck. You can imagine the rest. A romantic engagement against my parents' wishes. This was all shortly after the Second World War, and we celebrated the occasion with his pals. Small-time playboys, all of them. Once when he ran out of money I was stupid enough to stand surety for him. Never again! Take note: if you ever sign that kind of pledge, the bank has you in a chokehold. I finally realized that handsome Antonio was only interested in my fortune and turfed him out forthwith.'

'How did you come to have so much money?'

'If you're genuinely interested, then prepare to hear a German family saga.'

'Gladly.'

'But before I start I'm going to allow myself another Virginia. Would you have a light? So, this is what happened. My father Ferdinand fell headlong in love with my mother Feodora after the war and they married very young in Berlin. She was born a Feyerabend, meaning she was Jewish. Neither of them cared much about religion. I believe my father was pretty conservative, a highly respectable man. He studied at the Technical University and, after graduating, took over the running of a small company in Steglitz and turned it into a profitable engineering works. He quickly grew rich, and everything went swimmingly until 1933.

'The trouble was that my mother kept getting pregnant. I was her fourth child. I haven't seen my older brothers and sisters since. They probably emigrated or were murdered or simply vanished. I regret that I've never taken the trouble to discover what became of them, but I was far too small to grasp what was going on in Germany at the time. Your poor grandfather, who was three years younger than me, was also too young.'

'And then you emigrated?'

'It wasn't so easy. My parents hesitated for a long time because they thought that Hitler was a cartoon villain who wouldn't hold on to power. It was 1935 by the time the penny dropped. My father had to sell the factory under pressure and as quickly as possible. It was called Aryanization. Ultimately, my father was able to rescue just under half his fortune.'

'Where did they go? America?'

'To Amsterdam by train and then across to England. It wasn't easy to get visas and immigration papers for all the children. Mountains of red tape! And so they had to leave little Philipp, your grandfather, who was barely two at the time, in Munich with a distant cousin who didn't have any children of her own and did not object to the Nazis. They meant to have him sent over to England at a later date, but nothing ever came of that plan. The old battle-axe refused to return your grandfather, causing a rift between the American Federmanns and the Munich branch of the family.'

'No one has ever talked about this at home,' I said. 'Dad has always been silent about that period, and I've no idea what Grandpa did during the Third Reich.'

'Oh, Philipp can't help the fact that he was raised by a stepmother. A spell in the Hitler Youth, all those

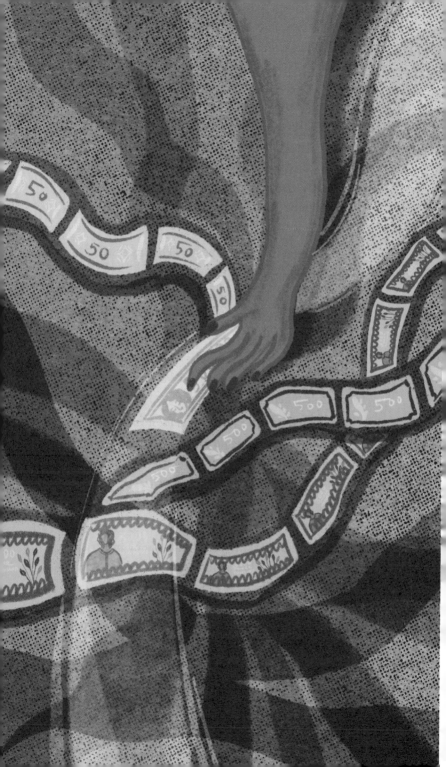

disgusting shitty-brown shirts, but no more than that! The main thing is that he wasn't a Nazi.'

'So how did your parents get on in America?'

'They arrived slap bang in the middle of the Great Depression. Do you know the song "Brother, Can You Spare A Dime"?'

'No.'

'I'll sing it to you. Maybe it will lift my spirits.

> *They used to tell me I was building a dream*
> *With peace and glory ahead*
> *Why should I be standing in line*
> *Just waiting for bread?*

Two pensioners stopped and listened open-mouthed. Aunt Fé's voice quavered a little—so the story *had* affected her—but she wasn't one to give up so easily.

> *Once I built a railroad, made it run*
> *Made it race against time*
> *Once I built a railroad, now it's done*
> *Brother, can you spare a dime?*

'I'm not quite Bing Crosby, unfortunately,' she said, winking at me.

'You were certainly better than Fanny in her show. But how did your life as immigrants in America continue?'

'It was a rollercoaster ride, with the economy going up and down. Then Roosevelt came to power with his New Deal. Things started to look up, and once again my father built a booming business. My parents bought a big house in Massachusetts, and they spoilt me rotten.'

'You don't say, Aunt Fé!'

'There's no need to be snide.'

'So what did you do after your studies?'

'My father died at the age of 53, far too young. First, he had to see his children through emigration before the Depression and, finally, success knocked the stuffing out of him. It's a well-known fact that success comes at a price, albeit not at as high a price as disaster. My poor father had always worked too hard. Not only was Mama tougher, but she was never concerned with money.'

'And what became of you?'

'Despite my good grades, they kicked me out of Vassar.'

'Why?'

'Because I didn't stick to their rules.'

'And then?'

'I'm not going to tell you. It bores me. Let's continue our walk. When will we finally reach Neptune? Is it still a long way?'

'We'll only walk as far as you're happy to. Before we get to that point, though, I'd like to hear more about your career. I guess you were ambitious.'

'I always left much to be desired in that regard. I never dreamt of having a regular job,' she said proudly.

'So you lived happily on your father's money.'

'While it was still fun, yes. But then I grew as weary of the New York bohemian lifestyle as I did of my lovers. That lasted for 10 years until I eventually married dear Archibald.'

'Who on earth is he? You've never mentioned him before.'

'Maybe he wasn't worth mentioning. He was nice, but some years older than my father. Just imagine! My friends referred to him as my sugar daddy. He was fairly rich and unbelievably tolerant, though. Not a word about my sporadic affairs! Everything was fine until he passed away peacefully at the age of 65. I was an independent woman at last. Just as *you*'ve always wished to be. I wanted to see more of the world.'

'Where did you travel to?'

'Lisbon, London, Brazil, France, the usual ports of call of the day. What is more, Archibald had initiated me into the secrets of the financial world, and I thought I knew enough about futures and foreign exchange to have a little flutter myself. It was fabulous fun for a time, but if you only knew how much money I lost . . .'

'If there's one thing I do know, Aunt Fé, it's that thrift has never really been your forte.'

'I poured money down the drain by the bucketload, unfortunately.'

'And that worried your mother.'

'Yes. I kept it up for a good long time until one day my path crossed that of an old friend of my father's, a famous cardiologist. We were no spring chickens—I was 50 and he was over 70. His name was Dr Leo Spitzer. We married, and it was absolutely idyllic! What more can I say?'

'And all of a sudden you were as good as gold?'

'And so was he.'

'Hardly surprising, given your age!'

'It's no laughing matter, my dear. It was tragic, in fact. He didn't want to give up his clinic and worked like a maniac. Then one day, after we'd been together for 10 years, my Leo dropped dead of heatstroke, completely out of the blue. I found him out on the terrace, far too late. Maybe it was my fault. I'd forgotten to put up the large parasol, but he flatly refused to wear a hat. I was inconsolable.'

'Late-blooming love. You never forget it.'

'How would you know?'

'But your financial worries were over.'

'Top-class doctors make a killing in America. I can no longer remember how much I inherited, but it was several million at least.'

'All in all, you had the Midas touch when it came to money.'

'What do you mean? That it was pure calculation?'

'Oh no, never!'

'You have a point, though. Love and money. One really shouldn't think too hard about how they may be related. Keep in mind that it's a minefield, full of traps and pitfalls. A wealthy woman never forgets that she has money—and nor does he. A wonderful subject for playwrights who earn their living from such conflicts, and for the lawyers who write pages and pages of clauses into loving couples' prenuptial agreements before they're free to stand before the altar, the registry office or the rabbi.'

'I think you have a lawyer like that too, Aunt Fé.'

'What makes you say that?'

'His name's Havelschmidt.'

'How do you know?'

'I'm not blind, you know.'

'He's one of a number of lawyers I employ, and he's the best. We're even on first-name terms. I call him Nikolaus and he calls me Fé. Saint Nicolas is the patron saint of lawyers—we Catholics know that kind of thing. Also, he is relatively honest, which is not something that can be said of most of his colleagues.'

'So you've had to contend with many lawsuits?'

'They'll sue you for a trifle in America, and then suddenly, for no reason whatsoever, you have to pay a few million. Compensation, alimony, disputes over an inheritance. These things rarely end well.'

'In your case they did, Aunt Fé.'

'I had more luck than judgement with both my husbands. When Leo died, I'd had enough of America and wanted nothing more to do with financial markets either. My mother lived in the family villa in Massachusetts until her death. She disagreed with my lifestyle, so I decided to return to Europe even though I knew very little about living here.'

'But not to Germany.'

'No, I preferred Switzerland. I moved into a villa on the shores of Lake Geneva. Why have you never been to visit me? It's very pretty there. You really should come and see me at La Pervenche soon. It's good to have your own home, because then no one can kick you out.'

'You'll never believe what Fanny asked me in all seriousness yesterday. She wanted to know whether everything that exists belongs to someone—those red-and-white poles on building sites, the pigeons on the pavement, the aerials on the roofs. Everything!'

'That's a very good question. Fanny's not as stupid as she looks. Did you explain the difference between possession and ownership to her?'

'Um, no. I didn't really know what to say. Who does snow belong to? Or a fence? Or the moon? And don't ever consult a lawyer: they only complicate matters. Often it isn't clear who calls the shots, even the experts can't agree. This river may flow through the centre of the city but it doesn't belong to the council. In this case, the federal state intervenes through its official bodies—for example the water authority or the regional environmental agency. The state can also lease out the flowing water if it so wishes. It has less authority over the riverbanks, though. Sometimes it's up to the municipality to decide, and sometimes a private landowner has enclosed it.'

'You appear to have read up on the subject.'

'All because of Fanny. I even got in touch with an agency with a particularly pretty title—the Department for Castles, Gardens and Lakes, a public interest administration which gave me a certain amount of access to their avenues and waters. It sometimes charges a small fee, but I'll gladly pay. I asked the chairman if he was also responsible for the pools, ponds and puddles in that little wood over there, but he just shook his head. What are the rules at your villa? Here, one may use the surface water without a licence, but not the groundwater.'

'My dear girl, please stop! If you had only ignored Fanny's question!'

My aunt began to struggle before we'd even made it to Saturn. She was a little out of breath. I realized that we had overdone it and would never make it to Pluto. There was a park shortly before the next bridge.

'How lucky,' I said, 'that we have one of those little phones you can't stand. I'm now going to call Herr Forster and ask him to drive you back to your hotel.'

The chauffeur arrived in record time. My aunt's eyes fell shut in the car. When we got to the Four Seasons, we gently picked her up and carried her to her room. I was shocked by how little she weighed.

When the rest of the Federmann family returned from their island holiday, my parents, brother and sister asked me, 'Did you spend a lot of time revising? The fridge is empty. Hopefully, you didn't forget to eat. Bozena will give the house a clean when she gets back from her holidays. And how's Aunt Fé?'

I had to tell them that Aunt Fé had vanished a week earlier. 'You know what she's like. She simply upped and left with no warning. No, she didn't leave an address. I tried to ring her in Switzerland, but with no success.'

And that was that until November.

III

AUNT FÉ MOVES IN WITH THE FEDERMANNS

After everything she had confided to me on the Path of the Planets, I was prepared for all kinds of unexpected events in my aunt's life. Accustomed as I was to her mood swings and quirky behaviour, I wasn't surprised not to receive any news from her and yet I didn't see her latest coup coming—not in the slightest.

She sent us one of her succinct postcards. This message had been stamped in Berne, although, somewhat curiously, the photo was of a steamboat passing the parliament of Budapest.

'I hope,' she wrote, 'that you have no objection to my taking advantage of your hospitality for a few days. I shall arrive with the train from Zurich at 11.28 on Tuesday. Perhaps Felicitas would be so kind as to come and meet me. Yours, Fé.'

My parents were bewildered. 'She wants to move in with us!' my mother remarked. 'How dare she!'

'Oh, calm down. The children will be delighted.'

'Ye-e-a-h!' Fanny cried, and Fabian too was overjoyed at the prospect of this visit.

'Why doesn't she stay at the Four Seasons if she's so rich? And how long is she going to be here?'

My mother had to ask Bozena to prepare the tiny guest bedroom for Aunt Fé. 'Oh my, this is like a broom cupboard. Isn't this too shabby for her? We'll need to fetch up the old bedside table from the cellar, and you're going to lend her your desk lamp for a few days, Fabian.'

The latter was by far the easier task because our cellar resembled a junkyard. A rocking horse, an old tape recorder, a clouded mirror and other bulky refuse the council wouldn't collect had been piling up down there for years. In order to provide our aunt with at least the bare essentials, the three of us had to rescue the bedside table—an heirloom from our late grandmother—from the chaos.

'And Bozena,' my mother called, 'please don't forget to put out a new bar of soap and some fresh towels.'

My aunt looked no different. She waved her cane cheerfully at me I had to fetch a luggage trolley for her two large trunks. They were heavy, made of the finest Russia leather with brass clasps and decorated with dusty stickers from hotels and ocean liners the world over. She also had an

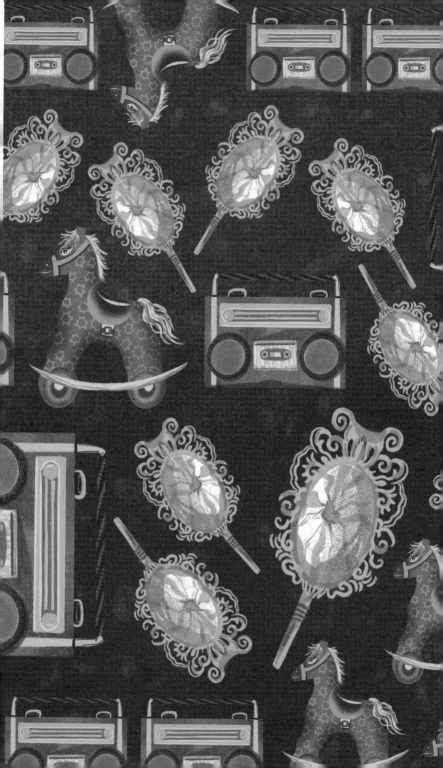

old-fashioned, monogrammed hatbox. I looked for the largest available taxi to transport her belongings and wondered whether the Turkish driver would be strong enough to heave everything into the boot.

When we got home, I pressed the doorbell long and hard. Our aunt hugged my mother and started unpacking her gifts for the family out in the hallway itself. None of them appeared to be recent purchases— they looked as if they'd been dug out of the bottom of a chest, the kind of place where you can be sure to find something suitable in an emergency. She hadn't forgotten Bozena either, presenting her with an incredibly long Indian scarf.

Once our visitor was safely installed in her quarters—this took a while due to the quantity and bulkiness of her luggage—a vague sense of bemusement settled over our family as we gathered around the coffee table.

'What do you think?' my mother asked. 'She seems pretty relaxed. Maybe she's taking a nap?'

'I could look,' I said. 'Maybe she needs something.'

The small guestroom smelt of mothballs. Aunt Fé had taken her eau de toilette out of her suitcase. I could see from the label that it was an old gentlemen's fragrance dating from the Second Empire.

By the second day she had made her little room homely. She was reading a French novel, *Dangerous Liaisons*, whose maxims for life she urged me to take to heart.

'Would you mind opening the window? It smells a little musty in here. Anyway, I can tell *you*,' she began. 'I'm broke.'

'I thought you must be. You wouldn't have moved in with us otherwise. But how did it happen?'

'Well, I was travelling a lot, so I left some bills unpaid. There was some trouble with capital gains tax, though I'll be damned if I even know what that is. The cantonal administration lodged a complaint. There's an agency in Geneva called the AFC. I have trouble keeping track of all these abbreviations.'

'You could have asked Dr Havelschmidt.'

'True. Of course, you know who he is, although I have never introduced you.'

'It's good to have a tricky lawyer to hand.'

'If it weren't for him, things would have turned out worse. But I have some other news for you.'

'Oh?'

'They've seized my villa. One day I found a polite little man standing at my door. He said he was the bailiff and would have to carry out his legal duty without delay.'

'That's some kind of court official. Here, they call him the man with the cuckoo. Why did all this happen? Because you owed your dressmaker a few francs?'

'Of course not. This is much more serious. An American court contacted the Geneva justice department with a request for administrative assistance.'

'Because you misbehaved in Massachusetts.'

'Nonsense. It is my dear old Leo who is to blame for this mess.'

'I can't believe that. He was always the ideal husband. As good as gold. You praised him to the skies on our recent walk.'

'Indeed I did. He was the best of men. But then I received this horrid official letter. A probate court in Massachusetts enquired whether I was the widow and heiress of Professor Leo Spitzer. A retired tradesman from North Adams, the letter said, had contacted them, claiming that the renowned cardiologist was his biological father. His lawyer had stated that his papers provided prima facie evidence of this, which is why he was contesting Leo's will. Mr Herb Bessie—that was the man's name—was now demanding at the very least his statutory share of Leo's estate, which was why they had sent a letter rogatory to the judiciary in Geneva, requesting that they seize material relating to Mr Herb Bessie's claims.'

'Wow, you already speak fluent legalese! Who on earth is this Bessie person?'

'Good old Havelschmidt has found out a great deal about him. He's a 70-year-old car mechanic from a devastated industrial town out in the middle of nowhere.'

'And that's why they hit you with a default summons, financial exactions and enforcement by writ?'

'Yes. The only thing the Swiss refused was to carry out the body search they also wanted.'

'So my father was right to call inheritance a bourgeois disaster. I'm really sorry about your villa.'

But Aunt Fé simply laughed scornfully and said, 'If it's no more than that! I've had to deal with this kind of thing a few times before. I'm not going to be browbeaten by some legacy hunter. Or the banks! *They* immediately blocked my accounts, of course. As long as they're convinced you're rich, they'll keep throwing money at you, but the moment you become a little strapped for cash, they issue threats and tear the shirt off your back.'

She went on to explain the distinction between default, a delayed filing for insolvency and bankruptcy fraud. 'It's very simple. If the wine merchant or the dressmaker sends you a bill and you delay payment, at some stage you will receive a reminder. You can throw that in the bin as long as you own your own home. That's not very pleasant, but it's how most rich people behave. They only block your accounts when your bank or the taxman starts bothering you. You are now insolvent, with creditors knocking on the door. But bankruptcy doesn't happen overnight—you can usually see it coming. What would you do in such a situation?'

'Oh please, Aunt Fé! How am I supposed to know?'

'Most wealthy people will of course have taken precautions long ago, such as stashing away a little nest egg in Singapore—a valuable painting or a few diamonds their creditors don't know about.'

'That can't be totally legal!'

'You can ask Dr Havelschmidt about it. He knows the criminal code inside out and would be glad to distinguish between a delayed filing for insolvency and bankruptcy fraud. I'm not very knowledgeable about such matters.' My godmother was a study in calmness. 'That villa was too big for me anyway. You would not believe the amount of junk that accumulated over the years! What am I supposed to do with my ball gowns from the 40s and the out-of-tune concert grand piano no one ever plays?'

I was in two minds about telling my parents about these latest, and fairly worrying, developments in Geneva. But they had long since drawn their own conclusions.

'I saw this coming,' said Dad.

'To put it mildly,' my mother said, 'she has become a millstone around our necks.'

The fact that Aunt Fé was facing the situation with such hideous insouciance only heightened their disgruntlement.

Fanny was the only one excited by the whole thing. She was desperate to know what Aunt Fé had in her luggage. 'Is there really only a hat in the hatbox or might there be a pile of money? And she must have hidden her jewellery somewhere!'

On Monday a letter arrived for her from abroad. It said on the envelope '*Recommandé à remettre en main propre avec accusé de réception*'—*Registered mail to be delivered by hand with acknowledgment of receipt.* The Kurdish postman was clueless as to what to do with it, but it brought an abrupt end to my aunt's reading and reveries. She calmed the almost illiterate messenger, signed for it and pressed the advice of delivery and a 10-euro note into his hand.

She steadfastly declined to comment on the letter's contents. That afternoon, she spent a good hour gathering her belongings before announcing her immediate departure. I ordered a taxi for her.

'Do you have enough money?' I asked.

She merely nodded and gave me an unusually vigorous hug and then she was gone. But where was she bound for? She wouldn't say, not even to me.

IV

AUNT FÉ'S LEGACY

The first snow had fallen by the time we heard from her again, but we didn't learn of her arrival via one of her customary postcards. It was Herr Stäuble who rang our home to announce that she was once more staying at the Four Seasons, what is more in the very same suite in which she had always so generously received us.

What had happened? By which miraculous twist of fate had the luckless woman been able to escape so swiftly from her creditors' merciless clutches? Mum was relieved that Aunt Fé wasn't reliant on our broom cupboard any more. It was clear that she no longer required board and lodging from us, but my parents still couldn't get over her rapid resurrection from financial meltdown.

'I'd like to know how she managed to pick herself up again,' said Mum, 'and you're the only one who can possibly find out.'

This I could not dispute. I had no doubt that helpful Herr Stäuble would arrange an audience for me with my aunt whenever I wished. She immediately had him ring up to tell me that she would be delighted to see me again as soon as possible.

I came straight out with my question. 'What's going on?' I asked. 'Where were you all this time? Why didn't you tell me the rest of the story about the thieves who were trying to rob you? What happened to your villa?'

She was as ingenuous, moody and generous as ever. 'Good old Havelschmidt saved me. First, he knocked back Mr Bessie and his lawyer. The documents they had submitted proved to be nothing but hot air, and their lawsuit was dismissed out of hand. But then the US Internal Revenue Service went on the attack,' she continued with a chuckle, 'and they tried to suck me dry. The IRS are a nasty lot. It's disgraceful that they even dare to call themselves a "service"! They sit there in their air-conditioned offices and claim that their terrorism is customer care. Anyway, they wanted their piece of the pie too. Thankfully, Havelschmidt negotiated a settlement or those bandits would have blocked my accounts for years.'

'So you still have a few million left over.'

'I don't know exactly how much I have, because then the Genevans clobbered me with inheritance tax. They don't hit you quite as hard as the Americans, thank God. Havelschmidt is something of an expert in these matters and he'll have arranged a good deal with them.'

'So you're living in your villa by the lake again.'

'Why don't you come and see for yourself?'

'I have to finish my flipping A-levels first,' I said. This turned out to be a mistake.

'I won't be able to visit Franz and Friederike this time, sadly. I must return home tomorrow to put everything in order. The garden's running wild! Pass on my best wishes to your parents, and Fabian and Fanny too. See you soon, my dear!'

The winter brought snowdrifts and black ice and seemed as if it would never end. No one but Fanny was up for the Carnival revelries in February.

Then one Saturday afternoon, shortly after Ash Wednesday, the phone rang. My mother answered it.

'Franz, there's a Dr Havelschmidt on the line and he needs to talk to you urgently.'

I listened intently, but I couldn't understand what the lawyer was saying. Dad's distraught expression didn't bode well, though.

My aunt didn't get to enjoy the luxury of relaxing at La Pervenche and recovering from the harassment she had endured. Her final adventure was death. She hadn't been as fit as she'd pretended for some time, but she hadn't been able to give up her expeditions. She wanted to climb higher and higher, and although she no longer found mountaineering as easy as she once had, she placed her trust in the technical aids she knew and valued from the past.

And so, one sunny day in February 2015, she had stepped aboard the funicular railway to admire the famous view of the Giessbach in the Bernese Oberland. This monument of Swiss engineering was older than my aunt and had discharged its duties to tourism ever since its construction in 1879 without the slightest complaint from its passengers.

Aunt Fé's destination was the old-fashioned grand hotel, perched proudly above the lake. Perhaps she longed to see the pointed turrets or the red balconies of the room in which she had stayed in her youth.

Yet just as the slanting carriages reached the dizzyingly high bridge over the waterfalls, her old heart gave out. If Professor Spitzer had been alive and on the spot, he would have known what to do, but the Chinese daytrippers chatting in the compartment behind hers looked on helplessly as she breathed her last, and by the time the train reached its terminus, she was beyond saving.

I hate funerals precisely because they are so utterly inescapable. Needless to say, the whole family was to gather beside Lake Geneva in order to pay our last respects. Since Mr Herb Bessie had turned out to be an inheritance hound, we were her only living relatives. When that is the case, the burial is held, as the language of obituaries, 'with next of kin only'.

The arrangements prompted long deliberations between my parents.

'The train journey to Geneva takes nearly seven hours,' Dad said. 'It's much quicker by plane.'

'Wouldn't that be extortionately expensive for the five of us?' Mum wondered. 'And what about the hotel?'

At this, I lost my cool. 'Carry on like this and you'll soon be discussing the price of the coffin and the wreaths. If you don't have any objections, I'm going to ring Dr Havelschmidt. He's never let Aunt Fé down.'

This, as it transpired, was the correct decision. It went without saying that his secretary would take care of everything, he said. As for the expenses, he would gladly advance the funds. As the executor of the will, he was not only entitled but in fact obliged to do so. Yet another curious expression! I knew that criminals were still executed in some parts, and it had also been explained to me that repayments and writs were executed or enforced. But here it was not atrocities that were under discussion, but benefits our aunt wished to bestow upon us.

'I have taken the liberty of booking a hotel for you. You might perhaps have preferred the Beau Rivage, but it is not ideally located and it would have been a tiresome journey to Céligny. I hope that you will be satisfied with this agreeable, somewhat smaller establishment on the lakeshore in Coppet. Should you wish to move around, there is always a taxi at hand. However, I will of course send you a car in good time for the funeral, which will take place at five o'clock on Thursday afternoon.'

My parents were greatly reassured by how accommodating Dr Havelschmidt was. Mum viewed this as an auspicious sign of how things might pan out from here, but our father merely shook his head.

'Who's going to give the funeral sermon?' she asked me. 'Your aunt wasn't very devout, but she was a Catholic, wasn't she? Isn't Geneva Protestant or even Calvinist? What are the chances of this going well?'

Although Aunt Fé did not have a very high opinion of the Church, I knew that she had never renounced the Catholicism of her youth.

'Don't worry. Havelschmidt has that under control too. He's arranged for a priest to rush over from nearby Nyon.'

''And what about the villa?'

'Mum! Please! There's no hurry.'

'Didn't you say it had been confiscated or seized or whatever it's called? Is everything in good order?'

'You'll have to wait until the opening of the will. That's what Havelschmidt the Omniscient says, anyway.'

Aunt Fé would probably have laughed at the sight of us all standing there in the small cemetery, our teeth gritted against the rain. She'd expressed a wish to be buried in the old cemetery in the wood, alongside a famous film actress who'd been a star in my godmother's youth. The busy executor had even been able to obtain this unheard-of privilege by providing the mayor with some financial advice. The City of Geneva's *pompes funèbres* spared no expense that afternoon. Wreaths and flowers were present, and the priest, a plump African man from Guinea, gave a consoling sermon in immaculate French, of which Fanny understood not a word.

The next day, Havelschmidt summoned us to the magistrate's court. The judge's chambers were a disappointment—the will was to be opened not in an ornate hall but on the second floor of a bunker-like building. Fabian and Fanny were not allowed to attend because they were under 18; our parents had to represent them. I was invited for the simplest reason imaginable: my aunt had left me everything. Everything, she had decreed by hand, 'is to go to my beloved goddaughter Felicitas'.

This was completely unprecedented in our boundlessly normal family. My parents had nothing to bequeath, nor were terms such as 'last will and testament', 'disposal of the estate' and 'the will of the testator' part of their vocabulary. As a child, I'd never even considered that the deceased might leave behind their worldly goods; I just thought they would look very white on their deathbeds. I understood even less, mind you, of the double Dutch uttered by the lawyers in Geneva. However hard Dr Havelschmidt tried to translate these texts, the clauses in the Swiss civil code left me feeling as helpless as a duck in a thunderstorm.

It was Saturday by the time all the obstacles to my first visit to La Pervenche were removed. Havelschmidt's secretary handed me a heavy bunch of keys for safekeeping. My family was visibly excited by the prospect of this trip. Fanny in particular clearly expected the surroundings there to put the Four Seasons in the shade, and it was certainly a very impressive place at first sight. The villa looked grand through the cast-iron entrance gates flanked by two stone columns. There was no doorbell, but the largest key did the trick. The taxi driver swung open both gates, and we drove up to the front door along a short drive lined with lime trees. There was no one to be seen, and only one basement window was lit.

No sooner had we stepped inside than a man we thought must be the butler appeared on the cellar steps— a short, muscular old man with a bushy beard. I recognized his rasping voice. This was the man whose curt replies had always scared Dad away when he tried to ring Aunt Fé. Monsieur Joseph, as he introduced himself, was obviously the housekeeper, for he immediately offered to show us around the house: the living rooms furnished with white-draped armchairs and divans, the conservatory complete with dried-out palm trees, the dusty kitchen, the ironing room and the cook's room.

An uneasy silence prevailed during our tour until Monsieur Joseph broke it to apologize. Her ladyship had been away for a long time and therefore not been able to put everything in order. The gardener had vanished some weeks ago, the chambermaid was working on her parents' farm, and their wages had not been paid. The unfortunate event had been so sudden!

A deserted house always makes for a depressing sight. Mum muttered under her breath that the kitchen was a mess—it required the attentions of someone industrious like our Bozena—and the parquet floor hadn't been properly waxed.

'It's a disgrace to let such a large house fall into such disrepair.'

She wasn't wrong there. The grand piano in the music room was out of tune, and the air smelt stale in most of the rooms. Some rooms looked empty, as if someone had already carted away the furniture. Even Fanny was disappointed. 'It was much nicer at the hotel,' she declared.

'Wouldn't you rather go back to Coppet?' I suggested. 'The taxi driver's waiting. I'll look around for a bit longer and then join you.'

'You're already acting like you own the place,' Fabian grumbled.

However, Dad understood that I wished to be alone. 'You probably have a few things to discuss with Monsieur Joseph.'

I quizzed the housekeeper before sending him home. It turned out that his real name was Giuseppe and he was from Calabria.

'I've been here for 20 years,' he said, 'and I can't and won't go back to my brother, who has five children. Here at least, I don't have to pay any rent. Everything within an hour of the lake is so expensive that I don't know where to go.' He looked at me with tears in his eyes. I had to confess that I did not intend to move into the villa. He need not worry, though. I promised to pay his salary and then asked him to leave.

The longer I wandered through the vacant house, the more uneasy I became. I'd always imagined Aunt Fé sitting at a Biedermeier escritoire, taking care of her opaque affairs and penning the occasional postcard. The desk would have a secret compartment. But I found nothing of the sort in any of the 23 rooms that were such a feature of our family folklore. I caught myself snooping for clues. Where were my aunt's documents, her passports, her pot of green writing ink? A photo album or a bundle of love letters?

The emptiness was scary. The only personal mementos were a dozen ancient dresses hanging in the huge, old wardrobe that dominated the landing. I sniffed them and caught a whiff of her *Eau Impériale*. But I'm not really into what people now refer to as 'vintage'. The labels, embroidered with names like Dior and Balenciaga, didn't appeal to me much either. Coming across a row of shoes, I wondered what to do with these relics. Adverts popped into my mind with messages such as: 'Inheritance? Break-up? Clear-out? We'll leave your house looking spick and span!'

It was so grim that I was on the point of giving up and walking away when I found an embroidered handbag in the coatroom that reminded me of Aunt Fé's first visit to our house. A few dollar bills, some loose change and a boarding card from the year before last; that was all. Those were the sole items I took home with me. I wanted to leave my aunt's secrets in peace and never visit La Pervenche again.

'I hope you found everything at the villa to your satisfaction,' said Dr Havelschmidt when I sought him out at his chambers to say goodbye. They were in the upper-class Champel neighbourhood, of course. Oil paintings hung on the walls, multivolume encyclopedias stood on the Empire table, and the lawyer had banished all computers to the outer office.

I've often wondered, without ever coming up with an answer, how my aunt came into contact with Havelschmidt. Of the 1,800 practising lawyers in Geneva, he was regarded as the star of his profession and his clients included major oil corporations, Russian oligarchs, hedge funds, politicians, sheikhs, even the odd dictator—all without causing any damage to his reputation. Lawyers in the world's third-most expensive city are referred to as 'Maître'. Although my visit was unannounced, he treated me with the same exquisite courtesy he afforded his richest business associate.

'It's about poor Monsieur Joseph,' I said. 'We'll have to find a solution for him.'

'You're right. In fact, we still have quite a number of matters to resolve. I fear that some of your aunt's furniture has gone missing.'

'This handbag is the only souvenir I've taken. I found no trace of her jewellery. I would have liked to have kept a ring or a brooch at least.'

'I am grateful to you for raising this sensitive topic, Frau Federmann. In recent times, which were, as you know, a little tumultuous, our friend, as I presume to call her, was forced to divest. She told me, word for word, that a woman of her age did not need very much. Of course, that ought to remain between the two of us, if for no other reason than Clause 163 of the SCC.'

'I don't have the foggiest idea what you're talking about.'

'It details what is known as prejudicial treatment of creditors by asset reduction. I can assure you that we have nothing to fear in that regard. In addition, there is the matter of inheritance tax. I apologize for troubling you with this. You presumably have a tax consultant to advise you. Ah, what was his name again?'

'You mean Herr Semmelschneider, who takes care of my dad's affairs?'

'In the unlikely event that the double taxation agreement were to prove beyond his capacities, he may contact me at any time. As for the villa, may I enquire whether you are thinking of retaining it for your private use?'

'No, I'm not.'

'Then perhaps we might envision a divestment. It is in a unique location, and local real-estate prices are high at present. There would certainly be no shortage of potential buyers.'

I was so exhausted by his explanations that I was sorely tempted to give him power of attorney there and then. The only thing stopping me was the thought of the shock this would cause my family.

'Have a pleasant journey home! My regards to your parents, your brother and your adorable little sister! You have my details, so please feel free to contact me whenever you like. Good luck and I hope to see you again soon.'

That, more or less, is how I recall taking leave of Aunt Fé's executor.

Aunt Fé's last will and testament was a great surprise, and my family had no choice but to embrace it. Dad, in particular, had no objections.

'See, Friederike!' he cried when we were safely seated on the plane home. 'What did I tell you? Fé always was a generous soul.'

'Yes, Franz, but she didn't spare a thought for the two of us,' Mum argued. 'Not to mention Fabian and Fanny.'

I should note that my brother didn't bat an eyelid when he heard that he'd been left empty-handed, and little Fanny merely shrugged.

'Felicitas will handle everything properly.' Those were the words with which my father shut down the conversation before it could get out of hand. I was convinced then, and I still am now, that time will prove him right.

The next ritual I had to endure was my final school awards ceremony in the assembly hall. The headmaster delivered a witty speech, the parents' association praised everyone and everything, most of the boys wore ties and the school orchestra played 'We Are The Champions'. I was cross because the report I brought home was not all *A*s, but my father comforted me by saying that he couldn't care less about marks.

The day after the end of school, a registered letter arrived from Dr Havelschmidt addressed to me. Peeling back his extremely polite cover letter, I found his bill. Despite their friendship, he had not executed my aunt's will free of charge. Quite a list it was! The hearse, the coffin bearers, the flowers, the stonemason, the donation for the priest, our hotel and the flights . . . It was never-ending. Along with miscellaneous taxes, levies and fees, he had of course not omitted his own remuneration—which was considerable. But I was, and still am, grateful to him for dealing with such a tangle of tasks on the testator's and my behalf. The remaining balance was still larger than in my wildest dreams. The most important piece of paper was at the bottom. A document with a red-and-white ribbon attached to it marked 'Certificate of Inheritance'.

This letter came with a carefully sealed small parcel. I opened it to reveal a small morocco leather strap with gilt edging.

> *Unfortunately, I was not able to impart to the three of you everything that I know about money—which was more than I would have wished. I hope that you will be spared that and will avoid following my example. I made so many wrong decisions! Incidentally, you should not take everything I said at face value. The less time you spend thinking about money, the better. There are many things in this world that will cause you far fewer headaches.*

Over the past few years, I have occasionally noted down other people's thoughts about money including lots of quotations, miscellanea and old adages. Flick through them from time to time, pick out the useful bits and forget anything that strikes you as rubbish. Feel free to underline a sentence here or there if it makes sense to you. You may even use it as an oracle—merely open the booklet without looking and point to a line at random. That's what the Persians do with their national poet Hafis, the Chinese with their I Ching and the gypsies with your hands.

Your godmother Fé

Quite some time has passed since I recorded what took place during Aunt Fé's visits and at her funeral. I read these notes with mixed feelings now. Sometimes I laugh, sometimes I marvel at how she toyed with us, the five Federmanns, how much she taught us and the things she withheld from us.

Fabian dropped out of his business course. He's studying geology in Norway. Fanny performs in pubs and has already built up quite a following among the cognoscenti. She improvises, dances and sings lousy songs. I don't know enough to judge, but we often talk on the phone and if she ever needs anything, I'll be there for her. As for my parents, there isn't much to report. My father has given up registering other people's cars. He receives a decent pension and builds miniature architectural models out of metal, wood and paper. My parents still live in the same house. My mother is still inventing new recipes and moaning about some ailment or other.

And me? I moved out a few weeks ago and am renting a small flat in Berlin. My interest in economics has waned considerably. I continue to keep half an eye on developments in the business world, but the feverish frenzy of rising and falling stock markets bores me stiff.

Just over half of my inheritance remained after I had settled Dr Havelschmidt's invoice and my tax bill. Dad warned me many years ago about the 'bourgeois disaster' an inheritance can unleash. He was right. I have now disposed of roughly one-fifth of my money. Some I have given away, always in accordance with Aunt Fé's maxim: only give to people whose face you can see, never to institutions. I have no wish to go through life an heiress.

Occasionally someone asks me what I plan to do with my money, but that's the wrong question. It isn't about what I do with the money, but what the money does with me. I don't need much, and what I do need I can earn by myself in good time.

I keep Aunt Fé's *vade mecum*, this wonderful little memento, in a safe place. The final pages of my account contain a few sample extracts. I do indeed dip into it every now and then.

FROM

Aunt Fé's *vade mecum*

To my family I am a monster because I do not earn
any money.
—Paul Gauguin

Money alone does not cause unhappiness.
The contempt of riches in philosophers was only a
hidden desire to revenge their merit upon the injustice
of fortune by despising the very goods of which fortune
deprived them.
—La Rochefoucauld

Wealth hardens the heart faster than boiling water does
an egg.
—Ludwig Börne

I'm not one to save money. Make it and spend it: that's
my motto. And there's not many as'll say that.
—Captain Meadows
in Somerset Maugham's short story 'Home'

Said Clever Dick to Cousin Mitch,
'I swear 'tis mighty funny
That in this world it is the rich
Who own most of the money.'
—Gotthold Ephraim Lessing

If everyone were rich, no one would want to row
the boat.

If the usual means of creating money shortages have no
effect, then one must introduce lotteries.
—Lichtenberg

Money comes hobbling in and goes dancing out.

Oh, Time, Strength, Cash, and Patience!
—Melville

A man without money is a wolf without teeth.

Because money happens to be the one thing in the
world that makes me lift up my chin, wake up a freer
man and approach others with a firmer tread.
—Lichtenberg

People disliked the fact that Lord Byron threw away his
money rather than increasing it.

An animal that cannot climb should not entrust its
money to a monkey.

Despising money is like toppling a king from his
throne. It is to be savoured.
—Nicolas Chamfort

Money sounds good, said the girl, but cake
tastes better.

Money says ne'er a word, and straightens what
is curved.

Money never goes to the gallows.

If money goes before, all ways do lie open.
—Shakespeare, *The Merry Wives of Windsor*

Though men who are rich have more opportunities
than others for losing money, they also have more
chances of making it.
—Balzac, *What Love Costs an Old Man*

Between avarice and profligacy, my dear,
lies parsimony.
—Balzac, *Father Goriot*

Money is as nothing between us until the moment when
the sentiment that bound us together ceases to exist.
—Balzac, *Father Goriot*

There is money; spend it, spend it; spend more.
—Shakespeare, *The Merry Wives of Windsor*,
Act II, Scene 2

There is something ill a-brewing towards my rest
For I did dream of moneybags tonight.
—Shakespeare, *The Merchant of Venice*, Act II, Scene 5

Those who leave the biggest footprint
are also gifted the biggest boots.
—Brecht

Having more credit than cash
Is how you get by in this world.
—Goethe

The Phoenicians invented money—but why so little?
—Nestroy

Avarice is its own stepmother.
—Christoph Lehmann, *Florilegium politicum*

Avarice is such joy, I think,
as to the thirsty brine to drink.
—Georg Philipp Horsdörffer

Avarice is like fire: the more wood you feed it,
the more it burns.

Avarice is never sated until its mouth is filled with soil.

A miser and a pig well fed
Are useful only when they're dead.
—Friedrich Freiherr von Logau

A miserly man is like a horse that carries wine and
drinks water.

Nothing so evil as money ever grew to be current
among men.
—Sophocles, *Antigone*

There where the most money lies, is the law.
—Lucan, *Pharsalia*

Money does not stink!
—Emperor Vespasian

A man's money places him on his feet.
—The Talmud

And the Lord said unto Moses: Go, get you down; for
your people have corrupted themselves. They have
turned aside quickly out of the way which I com-
manded them: they have made them a molten calf, and
have worshipped it, and have sacrificed to it and said,
'These are your gods.'
—Exodus, 2:32

It does not help a man to be pious if he has no money.
—Martin Luther

No sooner does the coin ring in the coffer
than the soul flies up towards its maker.
—Johann Tetzel

Shame is with poverty, but confidence with wealth.
—Hesiod

Money, the master of all affairs,
Can often make a no a yes.
—Hans von Abschatz

Even the wisest of men would rather welcome people
who bring money to those who carry it away.
—Lichtenberg

In German 'Geld' [money] rhymes with 'Welt' [world];
there could hardly be a more apt rhyme.
—Lichtenberg

Where money is the bride, the devil himself has laid an
egg in the household.

Such paper currency, replacing gold
And pearls, is most convenient: you can hold
A known amount, no sale or bartering
Is needed to enjoy love, wine or anything.
—Mephistopheles in Goethe's *Faust*

Money is beautiful—but requires a lot of work.
—Adapted from Karl Valentin's adage about art

Health without money
is a moderate fever.

When one has much to put into them, a day has
a hundred pockets.
—Friedrich Nietzsche

A lot of money leads to great sins, a little money to
even greater ones.